# MASTERS AND PEASANTS

# Masters and Peasants

Theodor Kallifatides

Translated from the Swedish by Thomas Teal

DOUBLEDAY & COMPANY, INC., GARDEN CITY, NEW YORK, 1977

All of the characters in this book are fictitious, and any resemblance to actual persons, living or dead, is purely coincidental.



Library of Congress Cataloging in Publication Data

Kallifatides, Theodor, 1938–
Masters and peasants.

Translation of BÖNDER OCH HERRAR.
I. Title.
PZ4.K147Mas [PT9876.21.A45] 839.7'3'74
ISBN: 0-385-09916-9
Library of Congress Catalog Card Number: 75-40746


Printed in the United States of America
First Edition

CONTENTS

## FOREWORD

"I have wanted to write this novel for several years, but until now I could never bring myself to put it down on paper. Since this delay is a part of the book and a consequence of its subject matter, I would like to offer an explanation: up until now I simply never had the courage.

I had to wait until I had enough distance from my subject matter to allow me to view it critically and without prejudice. At the same time, I could not let the distance become so great that I would be a stranger to the life I wanted to depict.

I believe the right moment has come. I can look back without bitterness. I have overcome the folly of being proud that I am Greek, as well as the folly of being ashamed that I am Greek.

This is not to say that I have become neutral toward my homeland. Quite the contary. Only now, having removed as many of the veils as possible, can I say that I truly love my country—which I have always wanted to say but never could.

The book takes place within a definite historical framework. Neither the people nor the events are fictional. Though I have taken the liberties I thought were necessary to keep from injuring anyone. The town of Ialos does exist. In Greece and in many other countries. That is my experience, and it is this experience that I want to communicate.

Why, then, call the book a novel? Simply because what I present here is my own picture of reality, and not reality itself. I can lay no claim to that. No more than anyone else can."

T.K.

MASTERS AND PEASANTS

# *Part I*

# IALOS

## THE FIRST MEETING

June 22, 1941. The news that the Germans were coming had brought the whole village out along the road. The children and the younger men had climbed up into the Hanging Chestnut in order to keep a lookout. They sent down reports on everything they saw. Every time a cloud of dust rose in the distance they would cry, "Here they come! Here they come!"

The older townspeople could remember crying the same thing in 1926 when General Kondylis led the coup that restored the monarchy. Professional criers were hired to walk the streets of the cities and towns and announce the great news: "He comes! He comes!" I.e. the King.

The children were let out of school and formed choruses that also ran through the streets crying, "He comes! He comes!" And he did. The King came. But he didn't stay long. In 1941, he was forced to leave again.

He came back in 1945, and again people cried, "He comes! He comes!" and that time the King stayed a bit longer. But in 1968 it was all over once more. A person can't help wondering which generation of Greeks will be the next to take up the cry.

But that day in 1941, the Germans were a long time coming. The sun was hot, and the chestnut tree gave the only shade. It was a strangely beautiful tree. Old, over four hundred years, they said, and large and mighty. It took three grown men to reach around its trunk. In the old days people called it simply "the Chestnut" and everyone knew which tree they meant. But then a confectioner—which in Greece is a somewhat suspect profession—

committed suicide by hanging himself in the tree, and ever since it had been called "the Hanging Chestnut."

The confectioner's profession was suspect because the people of Ialos, which was the name of the town, thought that all confectioners ate a great many sweets, and they believed that eating a lot of sweets would make a person homosexual. It was lucky for Hitler that the villagers did not know he loved pastry. It would have cost him a considerable number of followers and admirers.

Again the lookouts cried, "Here they come! Here they come!" But it was only a donkey with an itch, who was rolling on her back in the road, raising huge clouds of dust. When the donkey got to the tree she was given several kicks for having dared to fool the waiting villagers.

The village Schoolmaster was pacing back and forth wearing a black look. He was surprised that he couldn't overcome his impatience. He thought about Cavafy, the lonely Alexandrian poet who worried that the barbarians would never come, for what would the world do without barbarians?

The Schoolmaster smiled to himself. The Mayor, who had seen the smile, came up and whispered in a thirsty voice, "I hope they bring some German ass with them so we can have a look."

The German army was still an attraction. No one in the village had ever seen a German. The local Member of Parliament had, of course, but he was in Athens, preparing his speech to the nation. He thought the war was over. Now that Greece had capitulated, there was no longer any point in the world's opposing Hitler.

This view was shared by many Greeks in official positions. The Athens newspapers were full of editorials appealing to the Greek people to cooperate with the Germans. The newspaper *Estia*, which still exists, and which supported the recent dictatorship, wrote: "For Greece, the war is over. The Axis Powers will prevail."

Several other papers commented in the same spirit—*Kathimerina Nea*, *Kathimerini*, *Acropolis*. The last two are still being published.

The Schoolmaster was one of the few who did not believe that Hitler would prevail. For such a victory would mean that his whole life had been in vain. He believed in Truth, in Justice. He used to tell his students that the laws of history worked for truth and justice.

This manner of speaking had fateful consequences for a couple of those students, who came to believe that history was some kind of machine with enormous motors and that human beings were the fuel.

One of them came to school one day and told everyone he had had a dream about history. But the rest of the children had quite different sorts of dreams.

The hours went by and the Germans did not appear. The people were disappointed.

"Are those bastards coming or aren't they?"

They felt almost as if they'd been cheated, like a lover whose sweetheart fails to keep an assignation.

"We can't stand here and wait for them all day!"

Some of them headed for home, but halfway there they turned back again. "Maybe they'll come now. Now that I've gone home, maybe they'll come." The Ialites, as the villagers called themselves, had a tendency to detect conspiracies in other people and in nature. The weather in particular was a notorious conspirator. This was not because the Ialites suffered from a persecution complex but rather from a sort of Hercules complex. Every one of them was so important that he had a mass of visible and invisible enemies.

Crazy Lolos, the village fool, got the idea of running to the village and buying cold drinks, which he then carried back to the waiting throng. He sold them at a great profit, and when anyone objected to the prices, Lolos would silence him by pointing out that the village was close enough so that anyone who wanted to could run over and get his own drinks.

"Why should I sweat like a pine tree so you can have cold lemonade, you lazy bastard?" Lolos would say.

Pine trees do sweat quite heavily, and the resin is used to flavor wine—the Greek wine called retsina. Retsina also takes on the resin's light brown color, which makes a person think of a pine forest on a hot afternoon when the resin is drying on the trunks of the trees in tiny drops that glisten like tears in the eyes of the earth. For pine trees are the eyes of the earth. Lolos was emphatic in that opinion.

After another hour or so even the phlegmatic butcher began to get restless. He took out a sharp knife and stripped the bark from the twig of a mulberry tree. Mulberry trees are supposed to be good for making pipes.

The town Lawyer watched the butcher's hands, which moved methodically and surely and never made a mistake. They were obviously practiced hands. A shiver ran through the Lawyer's thin body. "He's going to kill someone some day," he thought, or rather realized, for it felt as if this had already taken place.

The sun went down. Under protection of dusk, the young people up in the tree turned to adventurous games. The people on the ground heard small, suspicious giggles, and the older people who couldn't stand for anyone to be having fun screamed, "Eleni, come down here this instant!" or, "Why are you panting like horses up there?"

Of course the young people did not come down. The chestnut had served as a sexual kindergarten for generations of Ialites. The dense foliage had witnessed a great many activities that the whole village would have given its life to see. Many a scandal had been averted thanks to the shelter of that tree.

Farther up toward the village, windows began to light up. The feeble, erratic generator that supplied the town with electricity was unable to maintain a steady current, and the light flickered as if it were wrestling with the darkness. For long moments the light gave up, and the village sank into the night like a boat, to reappear seconds later. Each time it seemed to have come closer.

Most of the people had already gone. Only the Mayor, the Schoolmaster and some children were still waiting. The others were already sitting at the cafés, and the backgammon and card games had begun.

Of the adult male population there were only two people who had not gathered by the road to see the Germans. Old Mousouris, who was the town's wealthiest farmer, and David Kalin, who was a Jew. David Kalin was one of the few people in town who knew what the Germans did with Jews, but the other villagers thought that David had failed to appear simply because he was a Communist. In fact David had gone away several days before anyone knew that a German outpost was going to be stationed in Ialos. His wife and children were still in town, but David had gone to the coast to find a boat to carry himself and his family to safety.

Old Mousouris never went out to receive people under any circumstances. He was used to having them receive him. Or come to him. When he heard the Germans were on their way he lit his pipe and said, "If Hitler were coming himself, I wouldn't budge."

Mousouris was now seated at his usual table at the café, drinking his evening ouzo, surrounded by his grandchildren.

The village had three cafés, all of them in the square. Oddly enough, they all operated from the same building, too. At one time it had been quite difficult for the waiters to tell which café any given customer belonged to.

As a result there were often misunderstandings and even fights. Fights in which the customers cheerfully participated. There were even those who intentionally chose tables that might be considered controversial. There would be an immediate altercation among the waiters, a scuffle would follow, and the Priest would curse everyone, and everyone would curse the Priest. Many noses were bloodied, many lips were split, many ribs were cracked before the Mayor hit on a solution. (He was not the Mayor then. He was elected because of this solution.)

The square was divided into three areas, marked off with white lines like traffic zones. Then the name of one café was written diagonally across each area. Now the customers knew where they were seated, and there was no reason for the waiters to make mistakes. But of course the quarreling did not stop completely. What had previously been open warfare was transformed into a series of border disputes. Still the situation had improved.

But another change had occurred as well. When the cafés acquired boundaries, they also, in some inexplicable manner, acquired different status. The café on the right, facing the church, became the upper-class café. There sat Mousouris, the Member of Parliament, the Mayor, the Lawyer, the Circuit Magistrate, the Gendarmerie Commander, along with their families and relatives.

At the middle café sat the land-owning peasants. At the café on the left, where the odor from the slaughterhouse was at its most pungent, sat the landless peasants and the workers. There were also a few people who circulated freely among the various cafés—the Schoolmaster, Crazy Lolos, and the Priest.

The Priest was a man whose authority had been in serious disrepair ever since the day he was discovered behind the altar heavily intoxicated, with tears in his eyes and piss in his pants. People could not depend on a priest who drank heavily in private and pretty copiously in public, too.

The Ialites had very little patience with drunkenness. Public inebriation was a great disgrace. The man should consume the wine, they said, the wine must not consume the man. A person has to control his passions and learn to live with them. Passions mustn't get the upper hand.

The Greeks are a moderate people in matters such as food and drink. Greeks even learn to be proud of their capacity to endure thirst and hunger. Of course they have had no choice. Generations of Greeks have been raised on wrinkled black olives, half an onion, a swallow of wine, and a scrap of bread. Generations of Greeks have died too young, but proud. The same need for moderation applies to the passions. Greeks have many passions, which they have to control if they're to keep body and soul together.

The Priest had become a priest in the hope that heaven would give him the strength he needed to gain some peace and repose in his vast bosom, which opened up in an immense embrace each spring and attempted to consume the whole world, particularly its women.

The Priest pursued women on an unprecedented scale. He could not look at a woman before his muddled brain had conceived a plan of conquest. And he possessed a remarkable intuition with respect to the realization of these plans. He sniffed out women's weak points, and his reputation had spread so far that when the Ialites discovered he was to be made their parish priest, they took action to prevent it.

They wrote to the Archbishop. But this old churchman smiled contentedly and murmured, "At last, a priest who is accused of chasing women." Most of his other priests had been accused at one time or another of chasing boys. The Archbishop made the appointment.

And the Priest made a magnificent beginning. In his first sermon he preached long and well about fornication and the like. In conclusion he said, "It has come to my attention through God's mediation (a euphemism for gossip) that this congregation believes me to be a man who has fornicated with the wives and daughters of many of his parishioners. I do not consider myself to be an angel, and the proof of this is that I stand here among you. Nor do I consider myself to be a lecher, and the proof of this is that I am now your parish priest. (Here he suddenly flared up.) In a word, I can think of myself whatever I like. But you must choose: either you decide that I am a worthy priest, or else you decide that I am a lecher and that all of you wear horns in every place where horns can grow. Believe what you like. The choice is yours."

The Ialites chose to believe that he was a worthy priest. But behind the Priest's back, and before God's eyes, they believed that he was a lecher. Which was not true. For the Priest had managed to get the better of his enormous appetites. He drowned them all in vast quantities of red wine, and then he married.

In the evenings when he came home drunk and tired he would go into the bedroom, sit down beside his sleeping wife, stare at her with bloodshot eyes and murmur for hours, "My salvation, my beloved salvation." He often fell asleep right there in the chair, and his poor wife, who was quite young, did not really know how to go about getting him into bed. There was always the risk that he would wake up, and then he would inevitably want to make love. But she couldn't get used to the idea of making love to the Priest. Because for her he was still a priest, a man of God. And it was made all the more awkward by the Priest's habit of screaming and moaning out loud during intercourse, which meant that the whole village always knew what the Priest and the Priest's wife had been up to. She could see it in their faces when she went out to shop or to visit her mother.

The Priest's wife had asked her husband to be more careful, but he could not, even though he promised to copulate in silence. "Making love without your voice," he said, "is like eating without your tongue. There's no flavor to it." But in spite of the social inconvenience, the Priest's wife could not do without the Priest's body, either. Especially not after making love, when the Priest's bosom would be overwhelmed by the white doves of peace. Tears would come to his eyes and he would rest his huge head on his wife's young breast. His beard was like seaweed, soaked with sweat and tears, and she always felt like a shore where men came and birds came and waves, and where they all grew peaceful and all fell asleep, and she fell asleep in their midst.

To feel a great love is not so difficult. It is much harder to be its object. The frail young girl was afraid of the Priest's love. She never really understood how his love for her could be so profound, but she was able to receive it. She was like a shore. Not a steep, rocky shore where the waves were crushed. But a soft, sandy beach where the waves came as waves and died away as peaceful streaks of water.

The Priest could cross the boundaries between the cafés without causing a sensation. But it would never have occurred to old Mousouris or the Mayor to move their asses to the left side of the square. Nor did anyone expect them to.

So the male population of the village spent every evening in the square, each man in his place, each man conscious of his place. And there they sat on this evening as well, after having waited in vain for the Germans. The evening air was heavy with disappointment, and even though they all pretended everything was normal, nothing was normal. The Germans had taken possession of the town before actually arriving.

There were not many amusements in the town. Now and then a traveling cinema might turn up, but that was very rare. The main event of the day by far was the bus that arrived every afternoon from the provincial capital. Coastal towns wait for the boat. Inland towns wait for the bus. This difference is by no means trivial, though it may seem so at first glance. A boat making fast to a pier is another thing entirely from the mere parking of a bus. The boat takes its time before landing. The passengers have a chance to look at the people waiting on shore. The first greetings are exchanged at a distance. The expectation is of a completely different kind from that called forth by a bus. A Greek who has waited for boats all his life becomes quite a different person from a Greek who has waited for buses. This also explains why nostalgic songs about home are usually written by people who have gone to sea or who have left their birthplace by way of the sea. Seafolk leave their harbor slowly; they can see their village or city in its entirety, and the picture clings to the retina. Bus people simply swing around the corner and suddenly everything is gone. Leaving a harbor is an adventure. Leaving a town square is merely depressing.

The bus usually came about five o'clock, and people started gathering in the square by four. They pretended to be playing cards or drinking ouzo, but in fact they were waiting. The real café evening could only begin when the bus had arrived.

A person with visitors was a little more self-important than usual. He would normally sit down with his guests and other people would come over to say hello. It made him the center of attention, and even if it lasted only one evening, it was a great event in a person's life. It was an honor to have visitors. People talked about you, for the village was curious about strangers. You could stroll about at random, systematically, and tell people about your guest, who always happened to be important, or who became so. Graduate students became professors, cadets became adjutants to the King, and simple office clerks from Athens became powerful industrialists.

It was a great day for the visitor as well. He was given renewed assurance of his exceptional importance. If he came to town five feet five inches tall he could leave it at least five feet nine. Women lie about their age, they say. That may or may not be true. But it was definitely true that the men of Ialos lied about their height. There was not a single male Ialite who was not taller than he really was.

An Ialite who went abroad often found himself to be among the shortest of men who voluntarily showed themselves in public. He would then comfort himself by saying that he was tall for an Ialite. True Ialites never compared themselves with anyone but other Ialites.

The Priest was tall enough to hold his own both at home and abroad. But he had never been abroad. He often dreamed of going and was one of the few who ever asked the Schoolmaster to tell about all the countries his tired eyes had seen. This did not keep the Priest from loathing the Schoolmaster. He thought the Schoolmaster ought to have been a priest, and that he himself should have been schoolmaster. "That little bastard was born to be a priest," he used to say to the right-hand cantor, who was his intimate friend.

There are two cantors in the Greek church—the right-hand and the left-hand. The congregation joins in the hymns only rarely, and only during Easter High Mass. In order to become a cantor a person often had to start as a choirboy, obey the priest in everything, help the priest's wife with the shopping and cleaning, and on top of all that he had to know how to read. Or at least these were the requirements for someone who wanted to become a right-hand cantor, which was somewhat finer than a left-hand.

The town's right-hand cantor had traveled this long road, but when he ascended his podium he forgot all his humiliations, all the things he had had to suffer. He looked out over the congregation from tiny eyes that were drowning in pouches of fat. The right-hand cantor did not have a very good voice, but he had found the right cadence, which was hard to do, and many boys from nearby villages came to study with him.

The left-hand cantor, on the other hand, was a man who possessed only one thing in life—a wonderfully beautiful voice. He knew it, too. It was the only thing he bothered to know. It would have been impossible to find a more lethargic individual if you had searched all of Greece. He belonged to that relatively uncommon category of people who can wear out a pair of trousers in a week just from sitting. It was only in church that anyone ever saw him stand.

The Ialites had long been waiting for the day when the left-hand cantor would fall asleep and tumble over at his post. But here they were mistaken, for he enjoyed singing. He could see on the women's faces that his voice cut right to their hearts, and he did not begrudge himself the pleasure of making the Ialites jealous. There were many men among them who would never have set foot in church if they had not been afraid that he would seduce their wives.

He knew this, and he looked at them as if he knew it, and of course the Ialites began a campaign against him in which they maintained that he mistreated his wife and was as jealous as Othello. But the campaign fell flat. Nothing had any effect against the wall of self-sufficiency that the left-hand cantor had built with the help of his high notes.

The Priest hated his left-hand cantor, but they sat together in the evenings at the café so that no one would be able to say that the church in Ialos was divided. Even the bell ringer was allowed to sit with them when he wanted to.

But the bell ringer did not come to the café this evening. He was up in the church tower keeping an eye out for the Germans. He could still see the Hanging Chestnut farther down in the valley and several shadows moving around beneath it. And suddenly when it was almost midnight and most people had gone home to bed, he saw headlights approaching Ialos at high speed. The shadows that had waited for such a long time just barely had time to leap out of the way of the German vehicles. The Mayor was almost angry. "Those bastards don't know how to drive," he screamed. "Or else they're scared shitless." But the Germans were neither. Their commander, Captain Wilhelm Schneider, had certain principles. One of them was: "One should never arrive in a place. One should simply be there."

By the next morning, the Germans were in town. They were to be there for four years.

## THE TOWN REMEMBERS

The town was called Ialos. The name means "shore," and since it was far from the sea, people wondered where the name had come from. Local historians who were eager for the town to have existed since time immemorial maintained that the name derived from a period when the sea actually extended all the way to Ialos.

According to the historians from nearby villages, the name had come about in quite a different manner. They claimed that there was once a man who lived in Salos—the town's original name—who had difficulty with the sound of s. This man eventually became mayor of the town, and he then changed "Salos," which means "commotion," "uproar," or "upside down," to "Ialos," which was easier to pronounce by half.

There is no reason to suppose that there is any truth to this story either.

The town's inhabitants called themselves Ialites, while the inhabitants of the other villages called them *samatatzides*, which means "troublemakers."

Ialos could be reached by two routes—from the valley and from the mountain, which was called One Arm, feminine gender. No one could remember why. One Arm was not an especially high mountain, but it was utterly naked except for a single tree, a fig tree that had been growing on the very top of the mountain for decades. It was very strange, this solitary tree. It looked as if the mountain had a single, outstretched arm. Whence, perhaps, the mountain's name.

A tree growing in this manner demands an explanation. According to village legend, the local saint once spent a night on One

Arm. He felt lonely, as is often the case with saints. It seemed to him that the higher he climbed the further he was from God. He was suddenly homesick for his valley, where he had grown into manhood and later also into sainthood. He prayed from the bottom of his heart for companionship, and God answered his prayer. The fig tree sprang up overnight, and it is quite possible that God put a certain symbolic significance into his choice of trees.

It was a fig tree from which Judas Iscariot hanged himself, and if we go further back in history we find that Timon the Misanthrope recommended that elderly Athenians hang themselves from fig trees. The fig tree has had a thoroughly bad reputation ever since. The people of Ialos believed, for example, that it was dangerous to fall asleep in a fig tree's shade. You woke up—if you did wake up—with a terrible headache and a feeling of drunkenness, which nothing would cure. You simply had to be patient and give the tree time to "withdraw its shadow," as they used to say.

In any case, it appears that the saint escaped with his life. As for the drunkenness, that's harder to say, though there is no denying that the saint made an extremely sober impression on everyone who annually viewed his mummy, which lay in a church that stood outside Ialos in an area of numerous fresh-water springs.

This church had been given a name that was an honest attempt to tie together classical Greek paganism with Christianity. It was called Our Lady of the Many Waters.

The only passable route into town wound its way through the valley, which had rich soil and a rich history. Many battles had been fought there, as there were many villages that laid claim to the valley's land and water.

These battles varied in nature and scope, from private quarrels that often ended in a showdown with a fatal outcome for one of the parties, to more traditional battles between the different villages.

The valley often changed hands, sometimes at night without a struggle. Since all of the villages had built their own dams, they could alter the flow of the river, and the river was the only boundary line that people accepted. Thus it happened that a man fell asleep with the rush of the river in his ears, and when he awoke the river was gone. And his land with it.

The river had no name. It was generally called the River. But people also used a certain amount of invective with regard to it, and it was rare that anyone failed to understand what was meant.

Thus the River was also known as the Big Faggot, and, alternatively, as the Natural-born Whore. According to the Ialite view of such matters, the only difference between a whore and a faggot was that faggots often had to pay their lovers, whereas whores got paid. Homosexuality, masculinity, and prostitution were the shame, the burden, and the comfort of the Ialite men. Homosexuality had claimed its victims, masculinity as well. The most recent was the village bootblack. He was a little weak in the head, but not completely. He could play chess and he played brilliantly. But otherwise he was a fool and an easy target for all the jokes and tricks people amused themselves by playing. The story of his fate was told with delight by the town's more advanced raconteurs.

Poulos, which was the bootblack's name, had died a hideously painful death after being persuaded that a man could maintain an erection forever by reinforcing it with concrete. Poulos had been quick to act on this suggestion, under the direction of the other men.

It was somewhat difficult to get him aroused right there in front of everyone, but they managed. Then they took cement and plastered it onto his erect penis, whereupon Poulos sat down in the sun to dry, as if he had been a raisin. He stared at the little rod between his legs and smiled.

When the cement was dry, Poulos couldn't get his pants on. His penis looked like a flagpole with a slight left-hand bias. But the men persuaded him to overcome his modesty and go out to the fields where the women were cutting hay.

Poulos trudged out during the afternoon break. At first the women could not believe their eyes. One of the jokesters had also hit on the idea of attaching a little bell to Poulos' trousers, the kind sheep wear. So when the women turned around to attend to a lost sheep—there stood Poulos.

Later, no one could say for sure exactly what had happened. The men found Poulos unconscious, bruised and bleeding, naked, farther down the road toward the sea. But the cement had withstood all the blows, and the women had attached the little bell to his penis. He died two days later of gangrene.

Men would do almost anything to be considered more masculine, and might do anything at all if they were not considered masculine enough. That was why the confectioner took his own life—out of desperation at being thought to be homosexual, and because he wanted to spare his sons that shame.

Between the death of Poulos and the death of the confectioner, the sons of Ialos grew up, continuously searching for the point at which masculinity becomes self-evident—and that point has always been falsehood and self-deception. Maintaining self-esteem comes to be identical with the ability to lie to yourself. Being a good person comes to be identical with having other people consider you a good person.

The chestnut tree, which remained innocent even after the confectioner's death, dominated the only passable road into the village, and it was along this road the Germans came.

The Germans would continue to come by this same route for four more years. While from the other direction, from the mountain, came the partisans, and the Germans could never find the secret trail they used. Because no such secret trail existed. The partisans came over the top of One Arm by summoning all their strength every time they came, and One Arm had claimed many victims. But the townspeople would never forget the day the blue-and-white Greek flag suddenly flashed from the top of the mountain, from the highest limb of the fig tree. And then disappeared again.

## THE MAYOR'S DREAM

The Germans had chosen to place a force in Ialos primarily because of its location. The town lay at the end of the valley. From Ialos it was possible to keep watch over the valley as well as the roads to the sea. And behind Ialos was One Arm, which was completely unforested and therefore ill suited to be a partisan hideout.

The inhabitants of the nearby villages expressed the situation somewhat more vividly. "The Ialites keep their eyes on the road. They eat from the valley and shit on the mountain."

The German detachment was not large and slept in the schoolhouse the first night. But the Captain, the Lieutenant, and two guards slept at the Mayor's. The Mayor was overwhelmed by this honor. And since it was one of his duties to represent the town, he had food and drink brought out even though it was almost one o'clock in the morning when the Germans arrived.

The German officers ate and drank but said very little. For that matter, they and the Mayor had no language in common. The Mayor knew a little French, but Germans have always felt that people should speak German. The two officers talked to each other and threw a glance at the Mayor every now and then as if he had been an article of furniture.

The Mayor appreciated this sort of treatment. For next to insubordinate underlings, there was nothing the Mayor hated more than evasive overlords. If a person was in charge, then everyone should know it. Such was the Mayor's reasoning, and he acted accordingly.

He mistreated his own people, despised them, and stole their wages, while toward the governor he behaved like an insect whom anyone might trample on and whom some people would not even deign to trample on.

No, the Mayor knew that life was a question of kicking down really hard and sucking up really well. That was the way to get places. And if a person had a few human lives on his conscience, what difference did that make? All human beings had to die some day. Why wait for God to call them? He could take a little of that burden from God's shoulders. In most cases it was high time anyway.

The Mayor was terribly eager for an opportunity to speak to the German officers. He wanted to ask them about Hitler. He wanted to know everything about the man, and, like everyone with a hero, he wanted to have his admiration confirmed. He had heard that Hitler demanded absolute obedience. That was attractive. How commendable that the German people had learned to obey. That was the kind of a people to be mayor of. Not these filthy damned peasants who pretended to be so grand and thought they knew so much. They would walk past his table at the café and instead of nodding and bowing they would sometimes even scratch their balls.

No, now they would see a thing or two. Hitler had come to town, and there was going to be law and order. The first law he was going to put through would turn the word "Communist" into a swear word. It would be illegal to call someone a Communist, and the guilty would be severely punished. The Mayor dreamed that in ten years' time people would know the word "Communist" only as a curse, at least as serious as threatening to rape everyone in a person's family including the ones who were dead.

The curses used by Greeks often deal with sex, which shows their preoccupation with sexuality and their aversion to it. The Greeks are not great lovers. In 1956, a study of married women revealed that 66 per cent had never had an orgasm. The results of the study were published in the newspapers and the whole nation went into mourning. There were bitter comments about Greek sexual ignorance, and the upshot was that one advice column after another began to appear in the papers.

Not many people wrote to these columns, for Greeks hate to ask anyone how to do anything, especially *that*. But the columns kept going on their own initiative and continued to spread valuable information, such as the importance of washing your feet before hopping into bed with your beloved.

"There are still many people in this lovely land," wrote one paper, "who do not know that water can be used externally. We often notice exotic odors on the bus, resembling everything from gorgonzola to dead snakes, and we are considering buying ourselves a gas mask."

It is not known whether the author actually bought himself a gas mask. But the Greek people did begin to realize that they had to start bathing and that they needed to learn something about the art of love.

In fact it was not long before advertisements for Greek tourism carried more or less open invitations to the women of other nations to visit Greece on account of the superior erotic ardor of the Greek soldier.

The Mayor dreamed of the day he would turn the word "Communist" into a curse, and he did not dream in vain. Eventually such a law did actually come into being, and it applied to the entire country. If a person had a grudge against someone he would go straight to the police and report him for slander, stating that the man had called him a Communist. And the police would arrest the accused person and question him closely as to whether he really believed that his accuser *was* a Communist, whereupon they might both find themselves in trouble. So the law did not have its intended effect. However, people could still have recourse to another law by which it was forbidden to call someone a "Bulgarian" or a "Turk."

"Bulgarian" meant the same thing as "Communist," while "Turk" meant atheist or non-Christian, plus generally dumb, stupid, retarded, or simple-minded. In one sense, "Turk" and "Bulgarian" could mean the same thing, namely, cruel.

No one was thought to be as cruel as Bulgarians and Turks. The Greeks have written their own history so that none of their heroes ever kills anyone unless he has the right to do so. But they are given this right far too often. The only Greek heroes who never hurt their country or any person but themselves are the Greek poets.

It is not known what else was discussed at this first meeting between the German officers and the Mayor. But it was not only the Mayor's windows that were lit that night. At the Schoolmaster's, too, lights burned all night long.

# THE CHILDREN OF THE KITCHEN

Ialos had the same division between north and south that is found in so many other towns and cities. But this division was not simply a geographical accident. It had social significance. The rich people lived on the north side and those who served them on the south.

No one knew any longer how this had come about. But the Schoolmaster, who often spent his free time pondering one subject or another, had reached the conclusion that it had to do with security.

"Nothing is accidental," he used to say. "Least of all in a Greek village."

The farther up the side of the mountain a man built his house, the farther he was from harm. The valley, on the other hand, lay open to human enemies as well as to the whims of nature. The River overflowed its banks periodically, and a lot of poor people had drowned or had lost their livestock or their harvests.

Another reason for building on the mountain was the view. The farther up you came, the better the view out over the verdant valley, or, in winter, over the River, which rushed toward the sea and grew steadily mightier and more dangerous. But of course the view was also useful. A person could follow the work down in the valley without moving from his terrace. He could watch his hired peasants, and if anyone was shirking it was easy to detect. Observations of the following type were often heard in the parlors of the wealthy: "That lazy Giorgos has gone off to piss for the fourth time in an hour. He's either got prostate trouble or else he's goldbricking. We'll have to replace him."

And the next day lazy Giorgos would be replaced, though neither he nor his replacement would ever find out why. They were not much interested in knowing, either. When confronted with apparently incomprehensible actions, the peasants always had the same ready explanation. They would quote the old proverb: "When the devil has nothing to do he fucks his own children." In the present case, this was supposed to mean that employers did what they liked.

However it would be an exaggeration to assert that everyone who was treated in this manner simply submitted without a murmur. The most recent ones to have protested were the dead confectioner's two sons, and they ended up in prison.

Their protest had been fairly drastic. They set fire to their employer's barn. His animals were burned alive, and an evil-smelling black cloud hung over the village for several weeks afterward. Some people still had nightmares in which they could hear the terrible screams of the donkeys and horses.

The employers were somewhat more careful for a while, but pretty soon they went back to their old habits. It would be a long time before anyone raised a hand against the rich or their property again.

Most mountain villages in Greece have a particular structure that might be called "hanging." The houses clamber up the side of the hill, leaning on each other, supporting each other, and leaving very little room for streets. This structure is due chiefly to the sloping terrain. At the same time, it is a means of social control. The neighbors know everything a person does. They can often see right into the house next door and overhear even quiet conversations.

In Ialos, this hanging structure was disrupted by the houses of the wealthy. They were built farthest up on the side of the mountain, and in front of each house was a garden. These gardens, which formed a sort of boundary between the rich people's houses and the rest of the village, were separated from each other by winding paths paved with large white stones that, while not completely regular, were nevertheless smooth enough to drive a car or ride a bicycle on.

The fruit trees in the gardens, especially the mulberries, hung over the garden walls, and the boys of the town used to test their courage by sneaking up during siesta time and picking the berries. They always picked too many, of course, and then threw a lot of them away on the stone paths. Later in the afternoon, grumpy, ill-tempered servants could be seen coming out of the rich people's houses with brooms and buckets of water to wash away the stains, which sometimes looked like blood. All Ialites were proud of this part of the village, which was called the Upper Town.

The middle part of the town consisted of the church, the three cafés, the shops, the government offices, and behind and around these, blocks of apartments where the civil servants and the shop clerks lived. The school had landed almost outside of town, and no one really knew why. It had been built with money sent back to the village by an emigrant.

The street that ran between the shops and the town hall was called the Promenade. The Promenade was the high point in the life of the town and a very dangerous place to visit. No one had ever made it from one end to the other with an unsullied reputation. The people you met, or those who had already taken up their lookout posts at one of the cafés, could always think of something you had or had not done.

The Priest used to stroll on the Promenade, but had given it up in recent years. He was sick and tired of having all the schoolchildren rush up to him the moment he appeared in order to kiss his hand—like a pack of wolf cubs. They had strict orders on that subject. No priest was ever allowed to pass unkissed. The adults would look on with satisfaction and then spit on the ground three times, for it was a bad omen to meet a priest, and spitting three times was a great help against bad omens. Everyone knew that. Some people maintained that the countermeasure was more effective if you pretended to spit on your testicles and at the same time muttered, "May I have your anathema, you faggot priest." But there was some disagreement on this point.

Yet this method did have its practitioners, and the Priest knew who they were. But there was nothing he could do about it. If he hadn't been a priest himself he would have done the same thing, and on those rare occasions when he journeyed to the provincial capital and ran into the higher "goats," as members of the clerical corps were called, he did.

In Ialos, unlike other places, gossip was not a pastime people turned to for lack of something better to do. Gossiping was considered almost a social obligation. It was the duty of every citizen to be well-informed, and at the same time it gave people a feeling of power to walk around knowing something about someone that he didn't know they knew.

It finally reached the point where everyone knew something about everyone else, although no one knew what was known to the others. And yet none of these backbiting, backbitten people was ever reluctant to pontificate at length on subjects such as morality, while their listeners would smile behind their mustaches, if they had any, or throw a glance full of insinuation at their neighbor across the table. And the person across the table would think, in turn, "Yes, I understand, you idiot. The man's an ass, but you're no better."

Of course whoever happened to be speaking was aware of what was going on and would think to himself, "Those two horse's asses think I don't see them, winking at each other the way soldiers wink at girls. But I know things about both of you it would make you blush just to think about."

This was the basic pattern of all conversations. Something was said that no one believed. Something was not said that everyone already knew. Finally, something was said to everyone except the person or persons it concerned. The people of Ialos learned this game at their mothers' knees. Naturally there were a few who never learned the game, and from their number society drew its heroes and its fools.

Every culture demonstrates a particular relationship to truth. There are cultures where truth is respected and sought after. There are other cultures where people assume that truth is precisely what everyone knows and where, consequently, people have no need to seek it. On the other hand they can modify it or adapt it, or transform it into something else. The Ialites took this latter view of truth.

South of the Promenade came the houses of the peasants. Their façades were blind, with maybe one or two small windows where, in the evenings, the daughters of the house would sit with all the vague longing that the girls of Ialos could conjure up. Their fathers and brothers were already sitting at their cafés, playing cards and drinking ouzo.

There was often a small vegetable garden behind the house. Some people even grew flowers. The woman of the house would sit there when she wasn't with the other women in one of their gardens or kitchens.

The peasant architecture of Ialos included no living room. The kitchen was the heart of the house. There people ate, there they sat in the evenings, there they discussed their family affairs. This was probably due to the fact that the kitchen was the only room in the house that was always warm.

Ialite family life emanated from the kitchen, and this fact had left its mark on men and women alike. Proverbs such as "Love begins in the stomach and ends in the bowels," struck terror into every Ialite girl. Ialite men invariably developed pot bellies, and since most of them were short-legged, they often looked like little kegs of beer out for a stroll.

Thinness was as horrifying a thought as open criticism of God or the King. No respectable man weighed less than 160 pounds, regardless of his height. The Schoolmaster was the only slender man in the county and was given a hard time because of it. Strange rumors about him began to circulate not long after he arrived.

Some people claimed that he was thin because he was a Communist and the Party had given orders to all Communists to keep themselves thin so as to be less visible. (Though this had had the opposite effect.)

Moreover, the Schoolmaster was not really an Ialite, although he insisted that the true Ialites, who could trace their origins back to Byzantium, lived in Asia Minor, from where he himself had come after the victory of the Turks in 1922. And he was partly right about that. All the same, he was happy to have come to Laconia, where Leonidas was born and where people had respect for the elderly and for men of few words—for laconic brevity.

But clearly these virtues too were born in the dim conceptual world of the kitchen. No human being can think clearly with a pound of baked beans in his stomach. The Schoolmaster was not disappointed by what he found in Ialos, but he was disappointed by the reception of the townspeople. In the beginning they were skeptical, later on they grew curious, and still later they began to hate him. Although no one could really say why.

The Germans were also children of the kitchen. How would it all work out? The Schoolmaster could not get to sleep.

## THE AWAKENING

Very early the next morning the town crier entered the Mayor's office. A few minutes later he came out again, took up a position in the middle of the square and announced in a loud voice that the German Captain would speak to the Ialites at ten o'clock that same morning and that all the townspeople were expected to be present.

The town crier was a little cross-eyed man with a stoop. But he had a really stentorian voice. He made his living as town crier, street sweeper, and occasional peddler. He would buy used articles and then sell them at a slightly higher price in the villages farther inland. But he made his big money on market days when he would challenge strangers' donkeys to screaming duels.

The crier and the donkey each screamed as loudly as they could, and the assembled crowd would then decide which one had screamed loudest and longest. The town crier never lost.

He had a nickname, acquired the same way other people had acquired theirs, that is, by saying or doing something that was found worthy of immortalization.

Anyway, one day the town crier had helped a truck driver back up to a store. The driver's rear vision was limited, so the crier stood behind the truck and called out instructions. "Come on, come on, your ass end's fine," he yelled, and the truck driver backed straight into the store and crushed a lot of merchandise. The driver was furious and jumped out and chased the town crier around the truck, shouting, "Come on, come on, your ass end's fine, you fucking faggot!"

Ever since, the crier had been called "Come on, come on, your ass end's fine." It was never clear whether he had misled the truck driver on purpose. In any case no one suspected him but blamed it on his being cross-eyed.

After a few minutes, newly roused faces began to appear in the windows. The Ialites did not like being awakened by the town crier. News could wait. The Germans could wait. It certainly wasn't necessary to go around waking people up in the middle of the night. But no one would miss the speech. That much was certain. No one felt he had any reason to fear the Germans, except David Kalin. And he had disappeared.

"Come on, come on, your ass end's fine," continued to shout as he wandered down the road through the village.

It was the somewhat more prosperous peasants who had built their houses along the road. These were the farmers who owned their own parcels of land, however small. The others, those who leased from the rich farmers or merely worked for them, lived a little farther down the hill in a tight group of small, whitewashed houses.

This part of Ialos was called the Lower Town, or Aphodilla, since aphodilla used to bloom in that spot. The emigrants who eventually came back from America called the Upper Town and the Lower Town "Uptown" and "Downtown."

Most of the emigrants came originally from Aphodilla, but their dream was to make their way into Uptown. This was a class struggle, of course, but not in the classic sense of the word. Those who lived in Aphodilla wanted to move upward, but they had no desire to take the place of the people then living in the Upper Town. They merely wanted to be included in their number.

What's more, it was the wrong classes that loathed and struggled with one another. It was not the poor against the rich, nor the proletariat against the capitalists. Because neither capitalists nor proletariat existed. Nor was there any bourgeoisie or peasantry. There were only rich peasants, small peasants, and landless peasants. The small peasants and the landless peasants were in conflict with each other, but toward the rich peasants they both turned faces full of respect and admiration.

Being rich was a virtue. Becoming rich was an achievement. Both virtues and achievements were valued in Ialos. It was not uncommon for the small peasants from Ialos to quarrel with the small peasants from other villages about which town had the wealthiest rich peasants.

This attitude had been implanted in the children, too. The poor carried on desperate campaigns of intrigue and flattery to persuade some rich peasant to be godfather to their children. And the rich peasants were not hard to persuade. They liked to have people owe them favors.

Constantine Richeas, a wealthy peasant with a wry sense of humor, used to say that there were lots of people in the village eating with his teeth. He was referring to the fact that he had paid dental bills for various people whose teeth had been knocked out in fights over the comparative wealth and power of the rich peasants.

The landless peasants struggled to get land and the small peasants to get more land. But it never occurred to anyone simply to take a rifle, build a boundary line with stones from the riverbed, and then say, "Here I stand and this land is mine and anyone who wants it will have to take it over my dead body."

Only generals could do things like that, and what would be the point of having generals if everyone could behave the same way? General Metaxas seized control of the entire country by just such means in 1936. In the early morning hours of August 4, 1936, he occupied the Defense Ministry and then issued this announcement: "Here I sit, and here I stay as long as I'm alive." The resulting dictatorship lasted for four years.

But the peasants were considerably more temperate. They didn't want to grab. They wanted the Lord to give them something for unpretentious living. A piece of land as a medal. They lived to be rewarded, either by God or by their earthly masters. This did not keep them from despising each other, trampling each other down, and in drastic cases even killing each other.

This belief in the eternal merit of the reward also protected those who were supposed to dispense it. The wealthy peasants could sleep soundly at night. No one coveted their wealth and power. The small peasant strove to be one of them instead, so that he could go to their dinner parties and stand in the front row in church and invite the priest home after mass and finally, perhaps, build a small chapel before he died, as a perpetual memorial. The people who passed by would have to stop and cross themselves and think, "This is his church. May God grant him absolution." And for a short while his memory would be forced upon them.

The landless peasants did not set their sights so high. You couldn't reach the roof without a ladder, so the ladder had to be acquired first. And the ladder was a piece of land or a good education. That was only possible for men, of course, who with an education might be able to marry upward.

Very pretty girls also had a chance to marry well. Beauty was not terribly common in those parts. Poor women started doing heavy field work much too early ever to have the kind of bodies commonly considered beautiful.

On the other hand, their bodies were mostly covered. So that when people in Ialos talked about a pretty girl, they were thinking mostly of her eyes, her throat and hair. The Greek poets never mention thighs and legs. Those are things they have never seen. But they write a great deal about long necks, black eyes, and blond hair. Because most Greeks are dark, blond-haired creatures are esteemed beyond all measure.

All heroes and heroines are blond, and those who were not blond to begin with have become blond over the years. Christ, for example, who had a head of curly black hair in the Byzantine period, exchanged it gradually for hair that was wavy and blond. The Virgin Mary met the same fate. Hence the modern practice of bleaching hair.

Girls who somehow got their hands on a little money would always invest it in becoming blondes. There was a story in the papers once about a seamstress who was so afraid of spoiling the color that for several years she never washed her hair. Suddenly one day she got a terrible headache, the worst she'd ever had. She thought she was dying. So she went to a doctor, and to his amazement he found a whole nest of cockroaches thriving under her upswept hairdo. He shaved the girl's head and washed her thoroughly with gasoline. The paper got its pictures, and the girl got rid of her headache. She later married a man who sold insecticides and he is said to have turned the roach story into a sales pitch and to have made himself a fortune.

Significantly, most blond children were born in the Upper Town. A few did turn up in the Lower Town as well, but that was unusual, and the mothers of these rare children were always unmarried—girls who had set their sights on the Upper Town but had not quite made it.

The most recent case involved a returned emigrant who knocked up a girl from the Lower Town. He had come home to choose a wife, and his dreams of the Upper Town were as vivid as they had been when he first left the village. Naturally he didn't choose the girl he had slept with. And the girl, at the prospect of having to live her life as an unwed mother, committed suicide. She poured gasoline on her clothes and lit it. The flames produced only a pale effect in the blazing sun. The emigrant married someone else, gave a little extra money to the church, and went his way. The Priest used half of the money for some repairs and put the other half in his private bank account.

"If we didn't live on sinners, who the hell *would* we live on?" he confided to his right-hand cantor. The right-hand cantor nodded in agreement, but later in the evening, sitting at the café with his friends, he told the whole story. His friends believed it, of course, but they also suspected that the cantor had had his cut.

It was common knowledge after all that the Priest and the right-hand cantor had formed an alliance against the left-hand cantor and the bell ringer. The bell ringer was a landless peasant who was exceptionally musical and could make the church bells absolutely sing. All the neighboring villages engaged him when they celebrated their saints' days.

But his art had an adverse effect on church attendance. Instead of going into the church, people stayed outside or took themselves to some hill from which they could better enjoy the bell ringer's masterful performance.

The bell ringer's service to God had made him somewhat deaf over the years, but he had not lost his incomparable sense of resonance and rhythm. The Priest and the right-hand cantor maintained that the bell ringer's deafness was God's punishment for some secret crime, while the left-hand cantor and the bell ringer himself felt that the Good Lord had spared him a lot of pain, since several hours or days of uninterrupted bell ringing would have given anyone else an earache.

It was not without reason that God's ways were said to be inscrutable. The bell ringer and the left-hand cantor felt that a person ought to make demands on God. But if he did, he became an atheist as a result. Neither one of them wanted to be an atheist. Neither one of them wanted to be anything at all that began with the prefix "a-." The grammar book said that "a-" was the negative prefix, and they were neither of them "negative people," as the saying went. On the contrary. They both liked women and children and wine.

The bell ringer regularly plundered the church of Christ's blood, which he then hid on the steep staircase to the bell tower. The sweet wine was quite safe there, because the Priest had vertigo and the right-hand cantor was much too fat to fit the narrow passage. Neither one of them had ever been in the bell tower.

The Priest often lamented this fact with the words, "I'll never get to see what that damned bell ringer sees." For word had it that a person could see right into the Mayor's bedroom from the bell tower, and that things happened in there that were well worth seeing.

The bell ringer reported that he had once seen an emigrant who was back home looking for a wife make love to the Mayor's eldest daughter, and he said he could not believe his eyes when he saw the man pull a little white balloon out of his pocket and put it on his penis.

"He could have blown it up and floated away," he told the left-hand cantor, wondering what it could have been. The cantor told him it was to make the man's penis stand up. As a rule, emigrants were no longer young men.

"You mean it's a sort of crane for the crown prince," as the bell ringer chose to express it.

The cantor thought this over in silence for a moment. "You might say that," he said. "But in order to use a crane you need a bigger crown prince than an emigrant has."

For one of the many beliefs about emigrants was this—that if you left Ialos and went abroad to make your fortune, and that if, in addition, you succeeded, your penis got smaller. All emigrants left Ialos virile men and came back eunuchs.

Nevertheless, the bell ringer had only increased respect for America, the fabulous country where such cranes were manufactured. "If I live long enough, I'll go there," he said. But he did not live long enough. In fact, he did not live long at all.

He must have had a premonition, for when he called the people to the meeting with the German Captain his ringing was filled with a desperation that was only barely disguised by the pure sound of the bells, reverberating through the thin air to meet the town crier's more and more weary admonition, "Everyone to the square at ten o'clock."

## THE SPEECH

By 9:30 the townspeople had all gathered in the square. Everyone was there except Mousouris, the wealthy peasant, who stayed at home, and David Kalin, the Jew, who stayed out of town. The shopkeepers closed their shops, which created a holiday mood. People wore their best clothes, as if it were important to put up a dignified front against the German domination.

But there were problems. The German Captain had brought no interpreter, so who would translate his speech? The Mayor recalled that old Stelios had been a POW in Germany during the First World War.

Stelios was also a seaman, plumber, gendarme, inventor, practical joker, storyteller—and much beloved. He had the town's biggest heart, with room for everyone, and his blue eyes, which had grown somewhat grayer over the years, reflected a life that had been filled with people and destinies.

Uncle Stelios, as everyone called him, was brought before the German Captain to be examined for proficiency in German. Uncle Stelios did not know much German, but he could tell several dirty stories in that language. In this manner he knew a number of languages. He collected stories, and through them, languages as well.

He told his first dirty story in Bavarian, and the Captain gave up, already smitten by the old man's warmth.

While Uncle Stelios took command in the Mayor's office, it was Lolos the village fool who dominated the scene in the square. He stood in the midst of a crowd of men and expounded eagerly his theories on German penis length. He was convinced that the Germans fell into the category "Pig Pricks."

The following categories existed:

1. The Chinese Diddle. Everyone knew the Chinese had little ones.

2. The Pig Prick. Not especially long, with a narrow glans. Considered to be particularly well suited to homosexual copulation and bestiality.

3. The Donkey Cock, or The Broken Arm. Long and thick, but not really rigid.

4. The Crown Prince, or The Wooden Leg. Long and thick, with a big round glans, and stiff as a board.

This last category was obviously the most desirable. But there were only two men in the village who could claim to possess a Crown Prince. One of them was Lolos—Panteleon in the church registry—but he had no benefit of his gift because he was the village fool and women were afraid of him. Lolos' organ was nevertheless much discussed, for a village fool is seldom a person but rather a sort of common property.

The other man with a Crown Prince was the Mayor, and his penis was often used to justify his position. No one had ever seen the Mayor naked, except possibly his wife, but it was a generally accepted proposition in Ialos that all leaders of all kinds must have large organs. This was because the townspeople could not tolerate a leader who was not better than they were in all respects.

For his own part, the Mayor hinted at this aspect of his person in his campaign speeches. "There are men who are men," he said, "and there are men who resemble men. I am a man."

Moreover he had eight children, of whom only two were girls. So his prestige was much too great for any opponent to overcome.

There was a lot of talk about female sex organs as well, and these too were divided into categories.

1. The Arch Crotch. Long and prominent and clearly visible under the panties.

2. The Chasm Cunt. So deep that not even a Wooden Leg was long enough to touch bottom.

3. The Little Dampness. Generally the possession of very young girls whose vaginas were thought to begin dripping slightly as soon as a grown man passed by.

Number One was the most highly prized, though the reason for this was a mystery. The hard-working old women who arranged marriages and who should and in fact did know everything about their merchandise could always say to which category the prospective bride and groom belonged. But naturally they improved upon the truth a bit.

Marriage for reasons of love or some similar emotion occurred extremely rarely. Since the stringent moral code made it impossible for the two sexes to have any contact with each other, it was also impossible for them to fall in love. The segregation of the sexes did give rise to occasional passionate affairs, but the rest of the villagers used these as cautionary examples. "He listened to his heart, and look what became of him," was a common theme.

Matchmaking was an institution made possible by puritanism, and no more zealous supporters of Christian morality existed than the marriage brokers themselves. They realized intuitively that the day girls and boys were allowed to meet each other freely and without fear, on that day the matchmakers would lose their livelihood.

The only man in town who had married for love was the metalsmith. When his wife died, quite young, he was left with two little girls. The metalsmith was a decent fellow, a capable, hard-working man. He was something of a braggart, but that hardly mattered. His modest insistence that he was the best metalsmith ever born on Laconian soil simply vanished in the general braggadocio.

He remarried fairly quickly, which was understandable. He couldn't take care of his work and his two little girls all by himself, so he did something about it. He married a servant girl he had met while making some repairs at the Pharmacist's.

The servant girl would come out to him in the heat of the day with food and wine. She made him coffee and used to sit with him for a while and talk. She asked about his dead wife and his little girls, and one evening when work was over the metalsmith lingered on. He looked up at the sky as if he were going to prophesy the weather. All he saw was a couple of sparrows and the servant girl standing at a window.

"Why should the world be so pretty when people are all alone?" said the metalsmith.

"To make them feel less lonely," the girl replied.

Two weeks later they were married. Wild rumors flew through the town. The girl had put a love potion in the metalsmith's food and drink. She had worked magic on him, bewitched and blinded him. He owned his own business, after all. How could he marry a servant girl?

The matchmakers declared full-scale moral war against the new couple. But the two of them held out. They held out until she became pregnant. She was a joy to behold. Her eyebrows were like two bridges, and her dark eyes shone out from beneath them like waterfalls at night. It was easy to see why the metalsmith got tears in his eyes whenever he looked at her. He called her "my pride."

When everyone could see that the servant girl was expecting a child, she disappeared for two days. Tongues began wagging again. The child was not his, she had run off in order to drown it, and so forth.

But the servant girl came back. It was a Sunday morning, and she came to church with her husband and the two little girls. She had her arms crossed on her heavy breasts as if she were leaning on a windowsill.

When mass was over and the congregation had gone out to sun itself in front of the church, the servant girl took up a position in the midst of the newly blessed Ialites and drew an old, well-polished pistol from her bosom.

"Hereafter anyone who makes an insulting remark about my husband, my two daughters, the child we are expecting, or me—he or she will get a bullet through the mouth. Do not forget that Captain Lambros is my godfather."

So spoke the servant girl, and people were frightened. The metalsmith whispered, "Come now, my pride, come home." And after that, no one said a word about them, at least not where it might be heard.

After all, Captain Lambros really was her godfather, and Captain Lambros was not a man people fooled with. He had once celebrated his son's name day by hanging twelve insubordinate peasants by their tongues.

The pistol exhibited by the servant girl, later the metalsmith's wife, was one that Captain Lambros had held in his own hand, and you might say it still smelled of blood. People realized why she had gone away. She had gone to Captain Lambros' house to get the gun.

"What a woman!" the Pharmacist sighed in the evenings among his medicines—his bottles and his tablets and his powders. "What a woman! What the hell was I looking at that kept me from seeing her?" This was a rhetorical question, for the Pharmacist knew perfectly well that what he had been looking at was the Mayor's maid.

The metalsmith and his wife won the only victory that love had ever won over the matchmakers and puritanism and ambition. The two of them were to become legendary, especially she, for the metalsmith became a legend early and early legends meet an early death. And die he did. He fell from the roof of a church he was repairing.

It was a little church, up on a hill. The metalsmith died instantly, but it was said that water burst forth from the spot where his head was crushed. This report came from two small boys who had gone up to the church to steal coins from the poor box and who had come back scared out of their wits and more religious than they had ever been before. One of them was later to become an archbishop and as such was famous for his merciless attitude toward anyone suspected of pilfering.

But this legend about the metalsmith did not live long, for it turned out that he had landed on a water main, which broke.

"His last repair job was a bust," remarked Crazy Lolos, and people laughed and the legend was drowned in their laughter, as is often the case.

But his wife lived and flourished. She grew prettier and prettier, and the men of the town were all crazy for her, and there was always someone trying to climb into her window. But she bought herself a shotgun and after that whenever a shot woke up the townspeople the same remark was made in many sleepy beds.

"Tomorrow we'll check and see who's running around with his trousers patched."

The metalsmith's wife lived to be ninety-four years old, and she was as pretty as a picture until the day she died.

The German Captain, the Mayor, Uncle Stelios, and two soldiers with submachine guns came out through the main entrance of the town hall. The Ialites, who were in the habit of applauding whenever the Mayor came through this door with visitors, clapped their hands. Uncle Stelios yelled at them.

"Cut the cheering, you idiots! These aren't Members of Parliament!"

The German Captain was confused. What sort of people were these villagers? The crowd grew silent. Captain Schneider took one step forward. Behind him were Uncle Stelios, the Mayor, and the submachine guns.

"It is strictly forbidden to be outdoors after twenty-four hundred hours without special permission of the German authorities. Translate!"

Uncle Stelios:

"Any of you bastards get the idea of running around town after midnight, we're going to cut your ass off."

Great applause.

Captain Schneider:

"It is strictly forbidden to possess and keep weapons of any kind. Including hunting weapons. Translate!"

Uncle Stelios:

"Any son of a bitch who keeps a weapon in his house is going to get the shit kicked out of him."

From the crowd:

"Hunting rifles too?"

Uncle Stelios:

"Up your hunting rifle!"

Captain Schneider:

"What did he say?"

Uncle Stelios:

"He wants to know if that also applies to kitchen knives."

Captain Schneider, directly to the crowd in hopes that everyone would understand:

"*Nein, nein!*"

Uncle Stelios, translating rapidly:

"No, no!"

From the crowd:

"What do you mean, 'No, no'?"

The Mayor, unable to contain himself:

"Keep quiet for Christ's sake! Fellow citizens, right at the moment it is very important that we keep our mouths shut."

Suddenly someone broke wind like a horse, or as the peasants used to say, "let a horsepower fart." The Mayor paused artfully and slowly raised his eyebrows, while Uncle Stelios put the situation into words.

"Who's the faggot who farted while the Mayor was speaking?"

"He said to keep our mouths shut, not our assholes," objected someone from the crowd, certainly not the guilty party.

"Fellow citizens . . ." the Mayor tried again, but he was drowned out by the crowd, all yelling at each other to shut up while the Mayor spoke.

Captain Schneider could believe neither his eyes nor his ears. He had never seen anything like these people. He threw a glance at the soldiers, who raised their submachine guns, and the crowd went quiet again. The Mayor was sweating freely, terribly ashamed of his people, while Uncle Stelios, deep down, was delighted at the story beginning to take shape. In his mind he had already begun to tell it, and to add embellishments.

By and by the speech was resumed and the Ialites were acquainted with all of the prohibitions that would henceforth apply. To sum it up, everything was prohibited except breathing. The Ialites were in a gloomy mood when they left the square and headed home to eat their dinners.

Uncle Stelios remained behind with the German Captain and the Mayor. The Mayor wanted to know if the German had really used the same phrases Uncle Stelios had used in his translation. The old man laughed.

"God damn it," he said, "a man has to have *some* fun out of being occupied."

## THE UNCONQUERABLE PAST

To be worthy of the name, every town, however tiny, must be able to boast at least one fool, one saint, and one whore.

At the moment there was no whore in Ialos. On the other hand there were quite a few fools—most of them unofficial, to be sure—and one saint.

The saint had been dead for a hundred years. He was not declared a saint immediately after his death. Fifty years were to pass before an enterprising mayor pushed through that decision.

The mayor in question had had a clear vision of the future. The news that Ialos had acquired its own saint and was going to build a church in his memory attracted common people as well as skilled craftsmen. And they came to stay, because work on the church continued for forty years without ever reaching completion.

The church was not noteworthy in any way, nor was it very expensive. But it was never finished, partly because the enterprising mayor died a sudden death when he fell off his mule and broke his neck, and partly because his successors were quite unprepared to carry on his project. Every mayor wanted to build his own monument.

One of them even went so far as to talk of building a school, but he didn't last.

For forty years the inhabitants of Ialos stared at a church that was only half done, and then someone came up with the fantastic idea of consecrating the church the way it was. Ruins were always an attraction, at least in Greece. So argued someone whose identity no one can remember, though it may well have been an emigrant who acquired his head for business in the States.

People laughed themselves silly when they heard his proposal, but when he developed the idea he got several people to go along with him. The subject was eagerly discussed, and it was finally decided to do as he suggested and consecrate the church as a ruin. It would have been better if everyone hadn't known when work on the building was begun, but they could always claim that the work had never involved a new church but only a restoration.

Moreover, many of the eyewitnesses were now dead and buried and could no longer open their mouths either to jeer or to object. Paradise is quiet, and in Hell there was far too much noise for anyone to make himself heard.

The people of Ialos loved silence and feared it at the same time. Nothing was so easily destroyed. People took every opportunity to make a racket, couldn't keep their mouths shut, and yet they had a terrible longing for silence. It was for this reason that Paradise was presumed to be quiet.

In any event, the saint's church was a half-finished building being promoted as a ruin. The saint's name was Ignatios, and many people felt that he must have been made a saint against his will. Otherwise he would have let the mayor, his discoverer, die peacefully at home in his iron bed, surrounded by children and grandchildren, rather than out on the street, under the hoofs of a half-crazed mule.

Ignatios had been a peasant boy. He grew the way a plant grows —lonely, trodden upon by every passerby—and eventually he became so shy that he took a job as a shepherd in the mountains.

There, during the long lonely hours when the sheep paid him no attention, he learned to play the flute. And he played so beautifully that the birds would come and sit all around him to listen.

But one day the young man had to go down to a village in the neighborhood to deliver five sheep to be slaughtered and roasted for a wedding. He took his flute, some bread and sheep cheese, and a little wine, and came down out of the mountains.

Along toward evening he came to the village, which was built on a high neck of land projecting out into the ocean and could only be reached by a narrow path. The town was full of wonderful smells—basil and geraniums, fried fish, meat, onions, the salt spray from the sea. Ignatios lingered in the square for a long time with his sheep. He couldn't get enough of the old houses, the pretty windows, the churches, the blue water breaking far below. But he finally overcame his enchantment and went to look for the customer's house.

It was a great palace, or at any rate the type of house that was called a palace. Three stories, with a lot of balconies and tiny windows. Ignatios should never have gone there, because there he saw the bride. She was sixteen years old, and he saw her watering her flowers with a silver watering can. He saw the flowers, and when she lifted her skirt to hop across a bed of roses, he saw her calf, and that was the vision he was to carry with him to his grave.

When he got back to the mountains, he could neither eat nor drink. All he could do was play his flute—for twenty-one days and nights. Eventually so many birds were fluttering around him that from a distance they looked like a brightly colored whirlwind.

At dawn on the twenty-first day, Ignatios died. But the birds stayed on. They picked twigs and leaves and buried him. The swallows were especially deft, for the swallow is the most skillful builder of all the birds. It was a grave worthy of Ignatios. No one could disturb him now. He lay surrounded by his birds, for they did not fly away, and hovering above them could be seen—by those who could see such things—the girl who had hopped over the roses, never doubting she would come to earth again.

The place was given the name "Bird Hill," and it was later to become even more famous when first the Germans and then the native Fascists used a nearby crater to throw their enemies into. No one knew how deep it was, and no one ever managed to find the bodies. Moreover, it was said to be identical with the crater into which the ancient Spartans threw their defective children.

Ignatios had lain there in the rain and the wind and the sun for several decades before he was discovered by the enterprising mayor, who needed an attraction for the town.

"Either a saint or a whore," he had reasoned. "Preferably both, of course." But whores were expensive, while a saint cost nothing. Furthermore, bringing home a saint was probably a better campaign stunt than bringing home a whore. Though it was hard to say for sure. In any case it soon became clear that a saint could bring whores with him. That is to say, when word went out that the people of Ialos were going to build a great new church and that they needed artisans and workers—and lots of them—the whores in Sparta smelled money and unfussy customers.

They arrived one Saturday evening in a rose-colored wagon on both sides of which large letters said PLEASURE PROLONGS LIFE, and under it, in smaller letters, *but it costs money*.

They parked their wagon in a secluded spot, though not so secluded that it couldn't be seen, and came out into the square and strolled about arm in arm like everybody else. The whores in Greece are ladies, especially to their customers. The customer must detect a wife in the whore or else he cannot enjoy himself. It made no difference that he had to pay for it. Good Lord, a person had to pay for so much in this life!

The other ladies in town were not particularly happy about the arrival of the whores, and a great many things were said in kitchens and back yards. But the men were pleased. One of the girls also knew an unusual variation called "French, Direct from Paris," which cost a little extra. Almost immediately someone decided to call this variation "smoking a pipe," as a result of which all the pipe smokers in Ialos had to put up with a certain amount of joking and insinuation.

Various venereal diseases spread through the village, of course, but no one took them seriously. The whores earned their money and the customers were satisfied. Saturday night was the night for love, though mostly for workers. Higher-ups usually went to the girls on weekdays. Even at the bordello, class differences arose. While workers achieved a certain status by saying they had been to the bordello, their superiors kept such visits secret.

Meanwhile, work on the church continued, the mayor was reelected, the women of Ialos resigned themselves to their fate, and the old women who arranged marriages went to the whores to get secret information about the single men. The whores became more and more involved in the life of the community. But they knew their place. They avoided shopping when the stores were crowded, and every Sunday they were among the first to church and everyone could see that they contributed generously to the collection box.

In short, sin was profitable. For those who practiced it and for those who permitted it. And everyone was happy and content—except for the girl who "smoked the pipe." She was not satisfied to be a whore and play the lady for her customers. She wanted to play the lady for everyone, and give dinners and celebrate name days. She tried every way she could think of to meet the townspeople socially. She bought candy for every child she met on the street, petted every dog she passed, had an appreciative word for everyone's mule. But nothing helped. The people of Ialos knew she was a whore, and that was that. One day the girl ran away, almost in tears. But after a while they heard that she was working at another construction site.

The other girls stayed on. They moved out of the wagon and settled down in a house they bought with their own money. The house was named for their runaway companion. It was called The Frenchwoman.

As the years went by, The Frenchwoman became the natural heart of the town at night. The men went there to drink and play cards and joke with the girls, and if they had any money they could go to bed with them too. If a man didn't have any money but did have what was called "face," that is, a solid reputation as an honest man who paid his debts, then he could sleep with the girls on credit.

Accounts were kept on the walls of the rooms with a piece of chalk. Walking into a girl's room, you could tell instantly whether or not she was generous. You had only to count the chalk marks on the wall.

By and by a doctor showed up and checked the girls once a week, every Monday morning. Regardless of whether any customers were present, the bordello madame would walk into the big room where the girls always sat and call out, loudly and clearly:

"All whores to bed! The doctor's coming to give you all a squirt!"

The first time it happened, the girls, who didn't know what it was all about, thought the doctor was going to make love to all of them. But in fact the doctor was utterly uninterested. He had only come to give them shots against gonorrhea, in accordance with instructions from the Ministry of Health. For there really was such a ministry, or at least there was a Minister who held such a post.

The Frenchwoman brought the town a lot of money. Men from other villages came to Ialos to have a look at the girls and even go to bed with them. This encouraged business and commerce, and everyone was happy and hoped that the church construction would go on forever.

But Ialos lost its whores for the same reason it lost so much else —because of the war. The whores decided they ought to move to the big cities, which were crawling with Occupation forces, with Germans and Italians.

## THE ABSENT SONS AND DAUGHTERS OF IALOS—MOSTLY SONS

As a result of the Occupation, Ialos lost another of its civic benefits as well—it's emigrants. The emigrants could no longer send money or come home from the States, and this cost the Ialites a good deal of income.

The emigrants were as much a living part of the town as if they had never gone away. People talked about them, knew what they were doing, took an interest in their aspirations, and weighed what they presumably would have thought about the town's various problems.

The emigrants had left the town in different waves, the largest at the beginning of the twentieth century. Most of them were landless peasants, but there were also a few small farmers. It was not only the young who emigrated. Men getting on toward middle age often chose to go to America, too. A man could earn money there, he could make a name for himself and then return to Ialos, drink ouzo at the American *pension* and play with his beads for days and nights on end.

The Mayor had forbidden minors to play with beads, partly because there was a feeling that the beads were only for adults, and partly because it was a Turkish custom with no basis in Greek tradition.

"Who the hell ever saw Socrates with a string of beads?" thundered the Mayor, who in fact had forbidden the beads because they got on his nerves.

Among the emigrants there were of course a small number of people who had left Ialos not in order to go somewhere else, but simply in order to leave Ialos. This kind of emigrant was not very common, but what few there were always remained emigrants, for they never returned. The town looked upon them as its black and lost sheep. They never sent money home, never wrote letters, and their families were ashamed of them and never mentioned their names.

And yet there were plenty of good reasons for leaving Ialos. Poverty, malice, and lack of solidarity among the poor made it impossible for any somewhat unconventional person to make a life for himself in the town unless he was willing to play the village fool. But these people were not fools. In actual fact they were the only ones who could see any farther than the ends of their noses, and such people are always despised and slandered and persecuted.

Emigrants of this kind seldom grew wealthy. They went to school instead and became teachers or engineers, married women from their new countries and rarely spoke of their homeland. But at the same time they were the only emigrants who ever owned any Greek books. Their homesickness lay deep in the marrow of their bones, for it was not a yearning but a wound that burned both itself and its bearer.

These men were ruled by the maddest dream a man can have—they dreamed of avenging themselves on an entire country. They often lay awake in their soft, foreign beds waiting for the message that would make their presence in Ialos essential. They would never go back until they were needed. But none of these people would ever be needed. Like any other village, Ialos didn't feel it needed knowledge. What it needed was money. And so letters went out from Ialos urging emigrants to come home, but not these emigrants. Restaurant owners, truckers, industrialists got letters. But never teachers and engineers.

The most notable of the Ialos emigrants was Georgios Kolonis, whose family name, which meant "to back off," came from a distant forefather who used to get drunk every evening and go out in the square and pick fights. When the other peasants failed to take his threats seriously he used to say, "Are you backing down, you coward? Are you backing down?" I.e., "Kolonis? Kolonis?"

So people began to call him Kolonis, and by and by it became his family name, although his present-day descendants spelled it as if it derived from the word *kolona*, which means "pillar."

Georgios Kolonis left Ialos as a twelve-year-old boy and all he took with him was a piece of black bread. When he came back thirty years later he had won the American Gold Belt in free-style wrestling, which was at that time the most popular entertainment in the States. His picture—arms outstretched, knees bent—was in all the newspapers, and in every newspaper it said in black and white that he had been born in Ialos.

This picture could be seen in every house in Ialos—the broad, powerful chest and shoulders, the bull neck and huge muscles—but on closer examination it could also be seen that a secret light burned in Kolonis' black eyes. It was revenge. His return to Ialos had become essential.

Kolonis was living proof that the Ialites were descended from the valiant Lacedemonians of old, the Spartan upper class with its famous wars and its strict physical training.

Kolonis became one of the greatest wrestlers in the United States. His popularity with the crowds was due to a special hold he had invented himself, based on techniques learned in the Ialos schoolyard.

This hold was called the Airplane Swing, and it consisted of picking up an opponent by the back of the neck and one leg, lifting him high in the air, spinning him around to pick up speed and then throwing him as far as possible. Kolonis always threw his opponent out into the crowd, and the crowd immediately gave him a good thrashing.

In the beginning, Kolonis was the only wrestler who could execute this hold, but gradually it became more common. It was said, however, that no one else ever quite managed to work up the same velocity. His battles with a Russian wrestler called Salkoff became famous across the whole United States. As a matter of fact Salkoff was also a Greek, but he had changed his name because, until Kolonis arrived, the ring was dominated by Russians.

Salkoff was also a great wrestler, and when the two of them met for the first time, New York society assembled it's most beautiful women and elegant gentlemen around the ring.

It was an even struggle to begin with, but eventually Kolonis managed to unleash his specialty, whereupon Salkoff, the supposed Russian, was heard to swear in genuine Greek that he would fix Kolonis and his whole family unless Kolonis immediately put him down again. Kolonis was a master of unexpected situations. He lifted Salkoff higher still, turned to the crowd and said loudly, "I was called here to fight a Russian bear. But what do I find? Ladies and gentlemen, I find a Greek lamb. Take him, tie a bow around his neck and let him graze peacefully till Easter."

And he threw Salkoff out into the crowd, which laughed uproariously. The next day the newspapers said that the sport of wrestling needed cleaning up. "We've got a lot of Greek sheep going around claiming to be Russian bears. This problem has to be dealt with before our rings get to looking like barnyards."

Salkoff vanished from the wrestling world. Kolonis reigned alone. He defeated Russians, Turks, Egyptians, and Persians. He made lots of money. Eventually he decided he would like to come back to Ialos, and by that time he could.

At the age of forty-two he left the ring and came back to his native village where he built a big house, fathered lots of children on three different wives, and lived to be a hundred and five. He also paid for a sports arena for the town.

But the vast majority of emigrants became neither famous nor wealthy. Many of them died at least as poor as when they left Greece, and many of them died alcoholics or criminals. Many of the girls became prostitutes. And there were many who didn't dare go back to their homeland even though they were almost overcome by homesickness. They were afraid of the devastating remarks of the villagers: "He went all the way to the States and still never amounted to anything."

The only person to have defied this law—the law that said the only excuse for having left Ialos was having succeeded somewhere else—was Uncle Stelios. He never got rich in America. He squandered nearly all of what little capital he took with him after selling his mother's farm, which was called Saint Peter and was one of the most well-kept farms in the region.

But he did buy a camera, and when he came back he could take pictures of the townspeople. Pictures of weddings, christenings, and funerals. Uncle Stelios would eventually grow rich in Greece, but he was incapable of handling money. People called him "the man with holes in his hands."

Emigration is an age-old phenomenon among the Greeks. Even in ancient times people left their cities and traveled off to Sicily, the Black Sea, the Turkish coast, and elsewhere. But since at that time Greece was a world power, those emigrants were called colonists.

Of course there is a difference, but it is not very great. Old emigration patterns still persist, and the emigrants have not changed. There are people who are out after money, people who simply want to get away, people who want to return some day, and people who never want to come back at all.

People who can't be outsiders, and people who can't be anything else, because they don't know themselves what they're seeking. But those who do know, know they are seeking a condition of total freedom, and total freedom always has its price.

What total freedom means, most of all, is freeing yourself from your own country, your traditions, everything you have learned to believe in and respect. It means leaving your own language and becoming forever mute. But there are some who come out on the other side of silence, who emerge beyond alienation and loneliness. And they are free.

Nevertheless emigration has changed its character over the years. In the beginning it was both a necessity and an adventure. In the old days people went out to conquer others, and now they go out to work for them. And yet however undesirable, emigration is a definite social alternative for the people of Ialos, and it always has been.

But the war and the Occupation would also alter emigration and the emigrants.

# *Part II*

# THE PYRAMID

## SHAME

The Germans made the Ialites ashamed of themselves. This was something only the German Occupation forces could have accomplished. Every German soldier was a living insult. The Italians were different. They aroused no shame in anyone. It is possible that this difference was the result of definite historical factors. It is possible that the Italians felt at home in Greece, for whereas a person may do as he pleases in his own house, at the same time he is never destructive, or scornful, or insulting.

But the Germans were all of these. The Ialites knew nothing worse than to be the target of German sarcasm. The soldiers walked around well-fed and clean and smooth-shaven, ready to snap to attention every time another German uniform appeared. They behaved like kindergarten boys out having a good time at the expense of the old and infirm.

The Germans had a way of pulling themselves up to their full height that made the Ialites feel ill. They had a way of laughing that made them feel as if a thousand knives were slicing through their bodies. And, finally, they had a way of walking as if they were moving among insects, not among human beings, and on streets and squares that human beings had built and loved and longed to come home to.

The vindictive character of the Greek resistance movement was a consequence of this shame that the Germans aroused in the Greeks. For the resistance had no great ideological content. The resistance leaders never clearly recognized this difference and they had to pay for their lack of insight later on.

The Germans lost the war, but in Greece the Nazis and the

Fascists won, and those who had fought against them were defeated. The resistance was discredited as nowhere else in Europe. Collaborators took over the government. Spies became the presidents of banks. Chiefs of police retained their posts and went on hunting Communists just as before.

It is easy to be wise after the fact. When a delegation from the Greek Communist Party went to Tito to get help during the Civil War, the old warrior asked them:

"What are you going to do with my weapons?"

"We are going to seize power."

"But you gave it away when you had it," Tito replied, and the Greek Communists received no help.

And that was certainly one interpretation. The Communists had their chance during and shortly after the Occupation. Afterward it was too late. But their failure in judgment had an ideological foundation—they believed in the capacity of their ideology to arouse the people, and they believed in the necessity of revolution. They were not shrewd enough to exploit the structure of Greek society for their own ends. And yet there is no getting around the fact that the Communists did organize and lead the resistance, even if they did misjudge its causes.

Very few men from Ialos took part in the war against the Italians or, later, against the Germans. A number of them did indeed enlist in the army, but only three of them ever got to the front—the three masons, with the sun on their shoulders. They were in it from the beginning as demolition experts. They had seen the war at close quarters while the rest of the Ialites knew almost nothing about it—only one nasty little song by an unknown poet.

The song was about Mussolini, who was very stupid, according to the song, for venturing to send his macaronis against the Greek lions. This song could be heard everywhere, and at any hour of the day or night.

The only ones who didn't sing it were the three masons, who had come back from the front gaunt, tired, and covered with lice. Their mother boiled their clothes for days, and the masons bathed for forty-eight hours before showing themselves around town.

The war with Italy had gone well but this was not entirely due to the bravery of the Greek army or the ability of its leaders. The Italian soldiers had been unwilling to fight. Many of them were opponents of Mussolini's regime. At that time Italy had one of Europe's strongest Communist parties, and the Party had repeatedly condemned Mussolini's war against the Greek people.

The three masons had seen the Italians wage war, and their impression was that they went into battle reluctantly. The Germans were another matter entirely. One platoon of Germans was the equivalent of at least two companies of Italians.

And in fact the Germans crushed all Greek resistance in a matter of weeks and won the war for Mussolini. The Italians could saunter to Athens as co-occupiers. But they showed no great zeal even as an occupying force. Instead of hunting down Communists and Jews, they engaged in commerce, strolled about town, and bought things to send home.

Eventually the Germans, too, got involved in this commerce and it quickly degenerated. Trade turned to pillage. After a few months there was neither food nor anything else to be had in Greece. The value of the drachma, the Greek currency, dropped daily and even several times a day. At the beginning of the war there were 22,000,000,000 drachmas in circulation. By the end of the war there were 6,279,943,102,000,000,000. A single piece of candy might cost over a million drachmas.

But no one in Ialos noticed all this until much later. At the moment it was only the three masons who had any sort of perspective. These three now sat at the Schoolmaster's.

The Schoolmaster and the masons knew what the Germans did with Jews. The Schoolmaster had read a little about it in the papers before the front collapsed, and the masons had wandered around in Athens, where with their own eyes they had seen terrified Jews selling everything they owned for a couple of tickets on a boat or a train. But where could they go? The only place left was Egypt on the other side of the Mediterranean, and it wasn't easy to get to Egypt.

The Schoolmaster and the three masons were trying to think of some way to help David Kalin and his family get out of Ialos. The hard-working Jew was not popular—perhaps because he was hard-working. But the Schoolmaster thought highly of him. David knew a great deal about plants and trees and always wanted to know more. He never mistreated his animals, and he raised his children with a gentle, loving hand. He sent them to school but had a private agreement with the Schoolmaster.

"Teach them Greek history and the Greek language. That's good for them. Teach them mathematics and physics, that's even better for them. Teach them about plants and trees. But let them have their father's faith—and they will be grateful to you forever."

The Schoolmaster, who had lived half his own life as a member of a minority—however privileged—among the Turks, knew enough to let the children retain their own culture and integrity.

The children went to school every morning well combed and dressed, two girls and a boy. They were pretty children. Their eyes shone with the loneliness that the Jews had been storing up for centuries. You could see from the way they moved that they had been raised in a quiet home, a home where voices were never raised. David's home was an oasis of silence in the town, though the other villagers mistook this silence for the fragrance of the honeysuckle that grew on the front of the house.

All three children were very intelligent. The younger girl in particular showed early signs of what the Schoolmaster called a gift for language. People were often amazed at the stories she wrote. Sometimes when the Schoolmaster had a different opinion about the construction of a sentence and complained that "that isn't the way it's said," the little girl would reply that she knew perfectly well that that wasn't the way it was said, that she didn't say it that way herself, but that a fairy tale might say it that way.

There was no point in reminding her that it was she who had written the fairy tale, for she knew that well enough. Little Rebecca, or Reveka as she was called by the Ialites, had discovered at an early age that there was a voice within her which in spite of its being hers was nevertheless not hers at all.

She used to take long walks by herself and look at all the flowers, especially the poppy, which she had heard was poisonous.

"To think such a pretty flower could be poison! And imagine laburnum being so dangerous to little children!" But she was no longer a little child herself. She could sit for hours under the laburnum in the schoolyard, alone with a voice that was not hers even though it was hers.

The Schoolmaster was very fond of Reveka, and so was his youngest son. Remarkably enough, this son had discovered Reveka's secret voice and asked her to read to him what she had written, for Reveka had begun to write down her stories and songs.

The two children would sit down under the laburnum, and as Reveka read, in her somewhat husky voice, the boy would dream of a distant land, far, far away, where he would go one day with Reveka and where she would read to him always.

In Reveka's songs and stories there was always someone she called Israel. The boy often wandered around by himself and talked to Israel, of whom he was jealous, because he thought Israel was a man.

"Is Israel dark like you?" he asked once, but Reveka laughed and said that Israel was a country, and countries were neither dark nor light. But the next day she told him Israel was dark. The Schoolmaster's son was light.

All three of his sons were light. Their eyes were various shades of blue, and their hair was chestnut brown. The Schoolmaster had been married twice. His first wife had died in Constantinople shortly after giving birth to a son. When the Schoolmaster came to Ialos, his first son was three years old, and he himself was thirty-two. Shortly afterward he married a girl just turned seventeen.

Despite her age, this wife soon proved herself to be courageous and mature. She came down solidly on her husband's side in his struggle with the peasants, which helped him a good deal. Her laugh and her Russian nose were famous in the village and gave her an authority that only people who are loved possess. She also gave life to two boys, at a six-year interval, which greatly increased the Schoolmaster's prestige.

"Three sons, three spades, three knives," the peasants reasoned. The spades were for the fields, and the knives for the family's enemies. But there was another way of counting too, the way used by Maria "with death at her heels," as she was called. "Three sons, three early graves," she used to say. A stroll through the village cemetery would reveal that this way of reckoning was also justified.

The cemetery, which lay a short distance down the valley and was surrounded by tall, slender cypresses, had seen the funerals of many young men, following one of the numerous wars, or after some private feud. Being a boy in Greece was honorable but risky.

Maria gave birth to six sons, and all six were killed. Maria, who wouldn't give in to death, gave birth to a seventh and dressed him as a girl. But he died too, although by his own hand. He was the confectioner who was accused of homosexuality, a rumor that began when the boy was still little and played in girl's clothes with his long, soft locks combed across his forehead.

Maria, who was very old by the time he died and sat mostly in the door of her house and mumbled to herself, fled the village. She took a few bedclothes and set up housekeeping under a bridge. There she died, after catching a terrible cold.

During her last days she used to go out in the middle of the night and stand on Mousouris' largest threshing floor where she would call on death and challenge him to a duel. But death never appeared.

"Death is a coward," was the conclusion Maria drew from this. "Death is a coward and refuses to wrestle. He sneaks up from behind."

Maria never got her duel. When death arrived, somewhat belatedly, she was barely conscious and could only repeat once more that death was a coward.

Maria's fate absorbed Reveka, and she took the Schoolmaster's son, Minos, with her on walks to the bridge where Maria's shadow could still be seen on the foundation. There was also a name on that foundation, chiseled into the largest stone. Stylianos Mousouris.

## AUTHORITY AND ATTITUDES

The town's leading personalities were two in number—Stylianos Mousouris, the rich peasant, and Charalambos Kostopoulos, the Member of Parliament. The Mayor liked to think of himself as their equal, but these two were definitely in a class by themselves.

The MP was related to the wealthy peasant. He had become a politician only after the death of his father, who was Mousouris' cousin, because the two old men would have nothing to do with politics.

"Politicians, ministers, and generals come and go," they used to say. "But the earth endures and waits for us all."

But the son was not listening. When the father died and the son took command in the house he threw himself eagerly into the political struggle, that is to say, into the struggle for a political career. But it was a difficult time for politicians. The generals had both the formal and the actual power. A civilian government did come into being on June 9, 1935, after a thoroughly rigged election in which he managed to get himself elected as the candidate of Tsaldaris' People's Party. But that government stayed in power only until the tenth of October that same year, when General Kondylis carried out his coup, restored the monarchy, and dissolved Parliament.

This was the same Kondylis who made the famous remark, "If I had known it was so easy to rule Greece, I wouldn't have waited to become a general. I would have seized power when I was a corporal."

But those five months in power had been enough for bold Charalambos. He had breathed the air in the corridors of Parliament, where power promenaded in a high silk hat. He discovered what it felt like to sit behind a big shiny desk and let people wait outside with quaking knees. He had nothing against the generals ideologically, but he did think they might have co-operated a little more with the professional politicians.

In any event he had now been unemployed since 1935, when he came back to Ialos and began living like a deposed political leader. His uncle the rich peasant looked at him with his uncommonly large eyes, so large they looked hollow, and said nothing. But his whole face expressed what he was thinking. "What did I tell you?"

The MP hated that look, but there was nothing he could say—partly because he had respect for age, and partly because he hoped to inherit a share of Mousouris' money. Moreover, of course, the old man was right. At least for the time being, for the young man had not given up. He took long, solitary walks preparing campaign speeches and a political program. Because now the people had awakened. Now a man had to have a political program.

It had been different in the old days. All a man had had to do was slaughter a couple of pigs and a few sheep at election time. Then when people were done eating and drinking he came out and promised them more than the Koran ever promised Moslems who died for their faith. The people didn't believe all the promises, but that didn't make any difference.

There was a story about an MP from a nearby village who was elected as a result of putting his foot in his mouth. He had finished a speech full of campaign promises, but since the applause was not as tumultuous as he had anticipated, he asked his audience to shout out the things they wanted and right there in full view and hearing of the whole village he would promise to satisfy everyone's needs.

It became a sort of auction, the people shouting in intoxicated chorus.

The People: "We want a church!"
The Candidate: "I will build you a church!"
The People: "We want a school!"
The Candidate: "I will build you a school!"
The People: "We want irrigation!"
The Candidate: "I will build you an irrigation system!"

The People: "We want a bridge!"

The Candidate: "I will build you a bridge!"

The People: "What the hell are we going to do with a bridge? We don't have a river!"

The Candidate: "I will build you a river!"

At that point the bargaining came to an end. The people started laughing, and the candidate thought he had ruined his chance of being elected. But he was wrong. What people were actually saying to each other was, "What spunk! He's the man for us. He doesn't flinch from anything."

He won the election easily over his opponent, who happened to be his cousin. This cousin went down in history when he said, after the election, "Any town that believes it's going to get a river is going to wind up without its daily bread." He never got to Parliament.

The political life of Greece differs from that of other countries in many important respects. But perhaps the most significant difference is that politics is not built around organizations like parties and labor unions and other kinds of associations with a political function.

Politics is conducted on a personal, individual level. The man who wants a political career is not reduced to serving coffee at the local office of some party or trade union.

Parties exist, of course, but most of them are temporary conveniences that last for the duration of one campaign. The trade unions never became powerful, despite the fact that Greece was one of the first countries in Europe to have a labor movement. Those that did exist were controlled by the police and the gendarmerie.

Politics as it is pursued in Greece means coming up with an occasional leader of really first-rate quality, but it also means paving the way for corruption and dictatorship. It is actually easier for one single man to establish a dictatorship than it is for a party.

Charalambos Kostopoulos, who was shrewd enough to know all this, conducted his politics in the old, accepted manner. He traveled around to the villages as often as he could, he christened crowds of children, he was best man at countless weddings, he promised a great deal to everyone, and he bided his time.

Shortly before the war he made a brief study tour to Germany where he attended a mass meeting at which Hitler spoke, and he came back with a new haircut. He also rebuilt the front of his house. He had all the small windows walled up and a balcony built like the one Hitler had had Speer build on the Reich Chancellory.

Charalambos would sit on his balcony in the evenings, gaze down the valley and dream of the day the people would stand beneath the balcony with their eyes full of tears and their hands raw from applauding.

To the peasants, Hitler was only a name. But to the few who knew anything, he was a very controversial person. Kostopoulos and the Mayor had Hitler as their ideal. The Ialos Gendarmerie Commander, having heard that Hitler began his career as a gendarmerie corporal, tried to comb his hair in the Hitler style, but without success. His hair was much too thick and stuck straight out over his forehead, with the result that people began secretly calling him "the eaves." The Mayor, on the other hand, was more intrigued by the fact that Hitler had no children.

The Lawyer, the Schoolmaster, the Pharmacist, and the Magistrate were against Hitler. Mousouris, the rich peasant, repeated as his opinion that only the earth endured. At the beginning of Hitler's war against Europe, the two camps used to make bets with each other. The Pharmacist, who had studied in Paris and who loved that city, thought that Hitler's farm boys would be stopped by the Maginot Line.

The Gendarmerie Commander, who had thought of himself as a kind of universal Chief of Staff ever since his promotion to lieutenant, drew maps on the tavern's paper and demonstrated convincingly why the Maginot Line would not hold.

"The Maginot Line is like a Frenchwoman," the Mayor used to conclude these discussions. "Holes everywhere."

Mousouris, the rich peasant, was old by then, very old. He made his way down to the square less and less often. But when he did he went straight to the table that was reserved for him and where no one else ever dared to sit. And he took his grandchildren with him, though only the boys.

"They have to learn authority," he told the family. "Authority is more of a habit than people suppose. You can't pick it up overnight. The Mayor may be the mayor, but nevertheless he's an ass."

Mousouris had grainfields, vineyards, olive groves, orange and lemon groves, gardens full of cantaloupes and watermelons. He had several barns with the best cattle in the region, and he had his own mills. He made the best wine in the area, and there was a great festival in the village when everyone gathered in Mousouris' barns to trample the juice from the grapes. The whole town would be there, with a single exception—the MP, who would sit on his balcony and watch.

It took three days to trample all the grapes, and the whole valley smelled of the juice. The flies would go crazy and wasps would gather from every corner of Laconia. The wasps loved wine must and were often drunk. They would go flying around picking quarrels, but the peasants knew how to deal with them. They covered themselves with netting from head to toe. Some of them even teased the wasps, who then tried vainly to attack them.

Mousouris knew that being a wealthy peasant made him visible, but he was a man who realized that if a person was visible he could not build walls around himself for people would only come and tear them down. No, once a man was visible he might just as well make himself even more so, but from angles that he chose himself. For this reason Mousouris would come down to the barns toward evening and treat everyone to a drink and stand and talk for a while. But he never sat down. He would be surrounded by his grandchildren as always, and his eyes would shine with the dignity that his family had battled and bled for.

He did not seek power because his power seemed self-evident. On the other hand he could not pass a pretty piece of land without stopping to let his eyes dwell upon it for a time. And then he would go to the owner and offer him a price.

People sold to Mousouris. Not because he paid better than anyone else, but because people knew that Mousouris would do anything to get a piece of land his eyes had dwelled upon. There was no particular point in trying to keep it from him.

But in general Mousouris wouldn't hurt a fly, and he gave a lot of money to the church even though he knew the Priest only put it into his own bank account. Mousouris owned a good deal of stock in the bank. So he was actually investing in himself.

Mousouris had been very strong and handsome as a young man.

But he had never slept with any woman but his wife, although there were many who desired him.

"It takes two lifetimes to get to know one woman," he used to say. "Why would anyone want more?"

Mousouris had his own ideas about love, as he did about land. He had little use for promiscuity in other men, even if it did consist more of bragging than of actual conquests.

The Mayor was his exact opposite. He claimed that every woman he loved taught him to love another.

"Women are like bridges," he used to say. "Once you start across a bridge you have to come to the other side. Only saints and idiots can stop in the middle."

His comparison of women to bridges may seem a little far-fetched, but it is important to know that the most famous bridges in Greek tradition are those that have somehow cost one or more women their lives. The ancient Greeks were in the habit of sacrificing a couple of women every time they wanted to go off to war and the wind was wrong. The modern Greeks retained this tradition in building bridges.

The most renowned was the bridge near Arta. It had forty arches. The men who built the bridge realized soon after beginning that it was an impossible task. The Master Builder was desperate until one night a spirit whispered in his ear that if he wanted the bridge to hold he would have to wall his own wife into the center pier. Eventually the Master Builder took this advice, against his will, and the bridge still exists, along with the song that tells its story. Freely translated, it runs as follows:

> Forty-five master masons and sixty journeymen
> labored day and night to build the bridge at Arta.
> But no matter how much they built during the day
> it all came crashing down after dark.
> The master masons grieved and the journeymen wept:
> Wasted is our labor, our drudgery for nought,
> everything we build by day collapses every night.
>
> A spirit answered from the highest arch:
> You will have no foundation to build upon

unless you wall in some living soul.
And do not choose some orphan, stranger or traveler.*
Only the fair wife of the Master Builder will suffice.

The song goes on to tell that the Master Builder was very upset when he heard what the spirit said and wrote to his wife and asked her to stay at home. The bird who took the letter, a nightingale, misread this letter and instructed the wife to come to the bridge.

She made herself pretty and went to the place and hailed the masons and journeymen cheerfully when she was still some distance away. But when she saw that her husband was sad, she asked the others why, and they confided in her that the Master Builder was sad because he had dropped his wedding ring in the middle pier and no one had the courage to climb down and get it.

So the brave, loving wife offered to go herself. When she reached the bottom of the pier she found nothing. At the same time the men up above began throwing sand and stones down on top of her, and her husband threw the largest stone of all. Thereupon she realized what was happening and sang as follows:

Oh what a fate! Oh what a destiny!
Three sisters we were and all die the same death.
The first upholds the Danube, the second, Avlon,
and I the last support the Arta bridge.
May the bridge tremble as my heart is trembling,
and as my hair falls out may those who cross this bridge fall off.

But they begged her to take back her curse on the bridge, for she had a single beloved brother who was away on a journey and who might cross the bridge himself one day. And the wife overcame her pain and altered her oath with these words:

Let my heart be of iron, and also the bridge.
Let my hair be of steel, and also those who pass this way.
For I have a single beloved brother
and perhaps someday he will cross the bridge.

* This would otherwise have been the natural thing to do. (Author's note.)

A real woman was prepared to sacrifice herself not only for her husband but also for her brother. If she had several brothers, then it was the eldest for whom she had to sacrifice. And later when she married and had children, she had to be prepared to sacrifice herself for her sons.

So the Mayor knew what he was talking about. And in fact everyone agreed with him, except for old Mousouris. Mousouris had great respect for his wife, who was one of those women who seem born either to walk on roses all their lives or else to die an early death.

She was pretty, intelligent, and wealthy. She was a queen. That was unmistakable, and anyone who made the mistake had occasion to regret it. She was so impressive that even a murderer might have kissed her hand before plunging a knife into her proud throat.

She and her husband had not had many children. Only two—a boy and a girl. The girl resembled her father; she had the same powerful body and large eyes. The boy took after his mother and was the prince of Ialos. He was as handsome as the sun. Tall as a pine and as lithe as a cat. When he rode through the village with a carnation behind his ear he looked like St. George. Only the sword was missing, but Mousouris' son was Mousouris' son and needed no sword. Moreover, he never encountered any monsters. Only peasants, their children and wives, and all of these people loved him. He rode on their hearts and he knew it.

If only people always did hate authority. If only it were that simple. The people had grown used to being underlings, or rather, they had grown used to having other people over them. It was a habit, like smoking, or anything else. A person can know that smoking is harmful and still love it and brag about his brand.

The people had other habits too. One of them, perhaps the most curious, was that they were dependable only up to a certain point, after which everything could change in a moment. And none of their masters ever knew exactly where that point lay. Otherwise revolutions would have been impossible.

Of this the Schoolmaster was firmly convinced—that revolutions were brought about by the masters themselves. Not by the people. The people took up arms, if they had them, only reluctantly. The people wanted to go on living the way they had learned to live—sowing their fields, reaping their harvests, growing into manhood and womanhood, getting married, having children (preferably boys), and then dying surrounded by grandchildren and relatives.

A solitary death was no real death. It was an agony. But the death of a person with many children was the beginning of a journey. There were innumerable folk songs on this subject. People lived close to death and looked on death as one of themselves. Death had a mother who was generally more merciful than her son, and he had a wife who whined like Socrates' Xanthippe and who grumbled when Death came home tired after working hard all day. But Death had no children. For Death was immortal and needed none.

> Mourn not the fortunate, those who die well.
> Mourn the unfortunate, those who die badly.
> Those who die in the midst of others do not fear death,
> but those who die alone tremble and are afraid.
> They look first to the door and then to the window,
> they look to the left and the right but see no one,
> neither a mother at their side,
> nor a father by their pillow,
> nor brothers nor sisters by their bed.

Death had his familiar implements—a scythe and a black horse. But he also had a snake. Not a big snake, but a small one called "the little star." This snake fed on the dead person's heart and drank from the dead person's eyes. In exceptional cases, Death might also have a bird, which was black like the snake.

The cross was often used as a symbol of the final suffering, in which case two small snakes would be crossed on the dead person's body. The underworld was also very evident in popular tradition.

> The underworld is evil, for there there is no dawn,
> the cock does not crow nor the nightingale sing.
> There is no water, and the dead have no clothes.
> They make their food from smoke and eat in darkness.

Daily life was thought to continue in the underworld, though under painful circumstances. In one song a dead man complains because he no longer sleeps under thick, warm blankets as he used to do. It is almost reminiscent of soldiers' complaints about ill-fitting underwear. But even in the underworld, women retained their beauty and their role.

> By death's waters, at death's small springs,
> three fair and captivating maidens bathe the dead.
> One bathes the sick, one those who died in their
> first childbirth,
> the third and loveliest bathes those who died of wounds.

These songs were copied down by the Circuit Magistrate, who would read them now and then to the Lawyer and the Schoolmaster. When they were together, these three often tried to identify what the Magistrate used to call the "spiritual focus" of the Greeks.

Was it death, or was it love, or was it something else? It was hard to decide. The Schoolmaster maintained that love played a subordinate role. The Greek, despite all the bragging he does about his conquests, is essentially a husband.

"Greeks are born with their feet in a pair of slippers," was the way he used to formulate this view.

The Lawyer, whose education differed from the Schoolmaster's (he was better versed in the Latin world) felt that the focus of Greek spiritual life lay in friendship.

"It is the only meaningful virtue, and it is dying out," the Lawyer would conclude his plea.

The Magistrate was, as usual, inclined to agree with the Lawyer, but nevertheless he felt that love held first place.

"Love—that is the tragedy of our people. We cannot live without it, and we cannot live with it. Only the Greeks can manage this ambiguous attitude. That's why we're all of us a little insane."

They discussed the subject at length without ever reaching any agreement. The Schoolmaster would not abandon his theory that the Greek was a husband, and the other two stuck to their theories also.

The Schoolmaster had come to the village in 1923 after the

Greek defeat in Asia Minor. He came to his new country, which in fact he thought of as his homeland, with eyes full of visions from the war. He had seen burning and murder and rape, and it seemed to him that there was little more of the world that he still needed to see.

He was short and thin, but tough. Unusually tough. Neither the Germans nor the Fascists ever managed to get any information out of him, in spite of all the torture he was subjected to. But that happened later.

The Schoolmaster wanted to live among the heirs of ancient Sparta. He wanted to raise their sons and daughters to be proud Greeks, but he found it harder every day. Pride had disappeared. There was no pride among the almost famished peasants. The pride was among their masters. But he could never walk in step with those gentlemen. The Schoolmaster was a socialist. He had become a socialist in Cairo, where he spent two years in a military prison during the First World War. He had been a Captain in the Turkish Army, which was allied with the Germans. The Schoolmaster had even been decorated by the Kaiser.

There, in the military prison, he had become a socialist. Socialism is one of the few ideologies that often spreads behind barbed wire and prison walls. With a certain gallows humor, old Communists often refer to prison as "the people's university."

The prisoners read a great deal, but most of all they talked. The Schoolmaster, Dimitrios Kalafatis, listened to all the conversations and read all the books he could get his hands on. He never went to the whores like the rest of the captured officers. He sat quietly by himself and read.

He learned English so he could talk to the guards. He learned to kill lice and bake bread. He began to play a violin that another prisoner had but couldn't play. He read Marx and he read Montessori and when he came to Ialos a great many ideas were boiling in his head.

But the townspeople liked none of these ideas. They even tried to burn down a little forest of pine trees that he and his pupils had planted. The Ialites did not want their children to listen to the Schoolmaster. But he didn't give up. He thought he knew how to deal with Greeks.

"As long as you persevere, as long as you stick to your guns, they'll respect you in the end."

And he was right. Nothing produced as much respect in Ialos as stubbornness. And the Schoolmaster was stubborn.

The Schoolmaster knew he would win them over eventually. It might cost him a great deal, but he would win.

He planted a school garden where the children all had their own plants to care for, or their own trees. He thought it was more important for them to learn to love plants and trees than to learn to conjugate verbs. All the children loved the garden, and all their parents hated it. But after a time when it became apparent that the schoolchildren got the best tomatoes, and the best melons and oranges, the peasants began to wonder about the Schoolmaster's methods. It was not easy to accuse him of witchcraft or they would have done so. No, there was no getting around it. The Schoolmaster knew his stuff. The townspeople began coming to him for instruction and advice. The Schoolmaster had won. The tough emigrant from Asia Minor had won. In the evenings he would sit at the café with the peasants, and even though he was no star at backgammon he was welcome nevertheless.

The Schoolmaster was one of two weak points in the Ialos power structure. The Priest was the other. The Schoolmaster because he had taken a stand for the people, and the Priest because he had taken a stand for his own body.

## THE FIRST PARTISAN

David Kalin was unable to find a boat. The news that he was being hunted by the Germans scared the ship's masters, who would otherwise have agreed to go since after all David was willing to pay and pay well.

Moreover, going out on the open sea involved great risks. There were mines everywhere; there were often air raids; the German patrol boats fired indiscriminately. Even the fishermen were reluctant to go out.

David was a Jew, and he looked just the way everyone imagines a Jew should look. But he was also a farmer, and the years of toil had given him the brown coloring of the earth and the bent walk of a peasant. Like all peasants, David loved his land, cared for it, and thought about it day and night. His situation was not like that of the Jews in the cities. David owned a piece of land that he wanted to hold onto and that his children would inherit. He wanted to see those children grow up among olive trees and orange groves. David would fight.

He came back to Ialos, hid in the valley for a couple of days, and then made his way into the town unseen. He went to the Schoolmaster. He knew the Schoolmaster would not hesitate to help him. The Schoolmaster had also been hunted and the Schoolmaster was also a stranger, though in his own land.

They discussed the alternatives—to stay and try to buy off the Germans or somehow bring them around, or to leave the village and take his whole family up into the mountains. At last they agreed. David would go into the mountains with his wife, while the children would remain in town. They would stay with the Schoolmaster.

"We are five mouths to feed," the Schoolmaster concluded the discussion. "Being eight won't make any difference either way. If my children go hungry, your children will go hungry. But not otherwise."

David was almost ready to cry. He knew the Schoolmaster would keep his word. The next problem was to get past the Germans and up onto One Arm. There were trails, which only a few people knew, but they were difficult, and they would have to go up at night.

One of the masons, the unmarried one, agreed to lead the couple. He knew all the trails, every stone, and every hole. He could climb One Arm blindfolded.

By the next evening, David, his wife with the honey-colored eyes, and the mason with the sun on his shoulders were up in the mountains, far beyond the Germans. David had a hunting knife and a gun.

When they came to the top of One Arm where the lonely fig tree grew, they stopped for a moment and looked down into the valley and on beyond to where the haze was beginning to lift. Way off in the distance was the sea, and beyond the sea were other valleys and other mountains, and all of it was Greek, where Greeks had lived and worked and died. No one must ravage that earth or dirty that sea. David patted his gun, kissed the mason, put his arm around his wife, and they continued on alone.

When the mason got back he found Ialos divided into two camps. One that either openly or secretly supported David, and one that was against him. The latter group was significantly larger. The Germans had told the Ialites about the worldwide Jewish conspiracy. The Ialites, who were not in the habit of thinking twice before believing things they wanted to believe, went back over David's life and of course found much that was incriminating.

Those who were against David cursed the idiot who had helped him get away. Those who supported David thought it was well and decently done. The Germans, who did not want to miss a chance of demonstrating the force of their prohibitions, chose three men by lot and sent them to labor camps outside Sparta.

Only for a month. But if it happened again, the Germans would not stop at forced labor.

This was communicated to the populace partly by word of mouth and partly by notices in both languages that were posted in all the cafés and outside the school, the church, and the town hall. Uncle Stelios had done the translation, and it bristled with curses. The Ialites grew even angrier. Some idiot had crossed the Germans and now they had to stand here and be told they were asses and horses' asses and congenital idiots.

David's house was confiscated, and the Germans had a couple of men from the village paint a huge Jewish star on the front wall, after ripping down the honeysuckle. But after a time they had some other men clean off the Jewish star, and Lieutenant Schultz settled down in David's house.

This Schultz also wanted to wipe out David's children, but the Captain, who was more sensible, let the children be. Provided they each wore a Star of David.

The stars were sewn on in the middle of the square where all the townspeople had been ordered to assemble. The three children trembled like leaves in autumn. Little Reveka was carrying her notebook full of songs and stories.

The stars were supposed to be visible from a distance of 100 meters, and several boys were sent running over to the other side of the square to report on whether or not they could be clearly seen.

Years later, Reveka wrote that she never in her life felt as naked as the day her star was sewn on.

The Schoolmaster kept his word. He took the three children into his home, but the masons insisted on helping, and in the end it was arranged for Reveka to stay at the Schoolmaster's while the boy, Marcus, moved in with one of the masons and the older girl, Judith, with another of the masons who was married and had children of his own.

Judith and Marcus took off their stars as soon as they came through the doors of their new homes, but Reveka kept hers. She would not take it off, she said, until the Germans were gone too. And everything else aside, it was a rather pretty star.

She slept in the same room with Minos, the youngest son. The boy was then seven years old, and the girl nine. In the evening when they went to their room, Reveka would say she was going to dress for bed, while Minos would say he was going to get undressed. When they noticed this difference they accused each other of saying it wrong. Finally they asked the Schoolmaster, who said that they were both right but that they got ready for bed in different ways. And that was true. Greek women avoid the word "undress," just as they always avoid drawing attention to their bodies, at least in the presence of men.

Reveka usually slept in a blue nightgown. Her skin had the paleness of a fresh honeycomb. When she fell asleep and the nightgown wound itself softly around her body, it looked almost as if she and her nightgown had grown into one.

Minos woke up one night from a dream. When he looked toward Reveka's bed he was surprised to see a blue light that seemed to rise from within her body. He had to feel it. He went over and put his hand where her shoulder stopped and her throat began. He could tell then that the nightgown was not her skin, but he could also feel a new warmth, a warmth he could never get from his own body when he put both hands between his thighs before falling asleep.

He stood there bent over Reveka and felt more and more certain that he would never be able to take his hand away. He stood still, and tiny drops of perspiration appeared between the palm of his hand and Reveka's throat, small wet islands in a newly discovered sea of joy and fear.

What would he do if they took Reveka away? He fell asleep beside her. He dreamed about a river, a vast river that he didn't recognize, and this nameless river ran not toward the sea but up toward the mountains instead. The river stopped where the fig tree grew, and Minos climbed up into it and looked down over the valley just as David and the mason had done several nights before.

Down in the valley he could see Reveka with some other girls. All of them had Jewish stars on their sleeves, and they all danced and tore off the cloth stars and threw them in the river, and the river carried them up to the mountain and beyond the mountain where the mountain stopped and the heavens began, and the sky filled with Stars of David and it was the most beautiful night Minos had ever seen.

Minos was known in the village by several different names. First of all he was called Little Liar. He lied about almost everything, which was a characteristic he must have inherited from his mother's father, the famous Uncle Stelios.

Secondly, he was called The Armenian, because the man who had been his godfather had had the same nickname.

Thirdly, he was called Meat With Hair On It. This was because he once refused to eat a soup called *patsas* which is made from animal stomachs and which is considered a delicacy and an excellent cure for a hangover.

Fourthly, he was known by the name Diridaua. The reason for this was not known.

Like his brothers, Minos showed early signs of possessing that imprecise quality called "being a great one for the girls," imprecise because it could mean either that the girls liked him or that he liked the girls. He used to run around naked, and he was the only boy in the village who dared do that. The Germans liked him because he had rather light hair, which also made his mother very proud of him. She called him her "prince," whereas his brothers called him "that little blond shit who always gets the best of everything." He had no memories before the Germans came to the village.

He had very little contact with his brothers because they were both much older. So he preferred Reveka. And ever since the night he discovered that her body generated a warmth that was warmer than his own, he would lie awake and wait for her to fall asleep and then put his hand on that same spot where her throat began its ascent.

He watched her artery and saw her blood pulsing back and forth in its blue prison, and he fell asleep with a fever sprouting within him, and the dream about the upside-down river returned again and again. Minos would search for that river the rest of his life. He told his grandmother about it, and she said he would be a merchant, because an upside-down river in a dream meant money.

## THE MERCHANTS

There were not many merchants in Ialos. Of those there were, only a few supported themselves chiefly on commerce, for most of the stores were owned by peasants who divided their time between their fields and their shops. One of the few full-time merchants was the man who owned the slaughterhouse. He was a businessman all day long. He traveled around to the villages to buy livestock, which was in short supply, and twice a week he came back to Ialos and had his assistant slaughter the animals and sell them. He had nothing to do with that part of the business. Along toward evening he would go to the butcher shop to collect the proceeds and then make his way to the tavern.

Cows and calves were seldom slaughtered; it was mostly sheep, goats, or pigs. Slaughtering had come to be one of the public amusements, and every Wednesday and Friday people would gather outside the butcher shop to wait for the ceremony to begin. They did not come merely to look. Old women brought baskets where they put the entrails that the butcher threw away. And the bones. You could always make a soup out of that sort of thing. Or feed your dog.

When the butcher came out with the animal there was an immediate silence. He wore a leather apron on which the blood had dried in dark red spots. He would straddle the animal, which naturally kicked and fought, and this act of straddling the animal and holding it fast with his knees made a strongly sexual impression, which very nearly aroused the butcher himself. His eyes would sparkle, and the women would follow the play of his thigh muscles with an attentiveness whose focus lay somewhere near the stomach.

The air smelled of blood and sperm. Then the butcher would raise his knife and plunge it into the animal's throat and the rape would be consummated. The women would let out their breath and plant their legs slightly farther apart than they had been before.

Hog slaughtering was probably the most popular. The butcher would stuff a lemon in the pig's mouth so it couldn't squeal, crush the back of its head with a heavy hammer, and then open its throat with a long knife.

Next the animal had to be skinned. This job could take a long time, but for the butcher in Ialos it was the work of a few minutes. His hands worked as if by themselves. Finally the butchered animal was hung head down from the roof of the slaughterhouse and everyone could start to buy. The butcher changed knives, placed himself beside the animal with his legs wide apart, and waited for bids.

The butcher, whose name was Christos, was a very large, strong man. As he walked around town, always followed by a swarm of cattle flies, he was reminiscent of the mythical Orestes. Christos must have inherited his unusual strength from his father, who was rumored to be the famous wrestler Kolonis, although nobody could ever prove it. In any case, the butcher was alone on earth. He had no parents and no relatives. The traveling merchant began taking him along on his trips because he needed a guard who could protect him from possible thieves, it being common knowledge that the merchant went about with quite a lot of money in his wallet.

But Christos had demonstrated his butchering talents early on. The merchant and he were out on business and happened to come upon an unskillful butcher tackling a well-fed pig. The pig screamed so loud it could be heard all the way to the provincial capital, where the archbishop woke up with a curse . . . But that is another story.

Young Christos stepped forward and, with the authority given him by his uncommon strength, he upbraided the clumsy butcher. Then he took charge of the pig himself and had it butchered and dressed before anyone could breathe twice.

Christos was to become the most famous butcher in the region. Young men came from other villages to observe his art. They would ask him to explain what he did, and he used to answer that it was all in the arm, which was the only answer he could give.

The slaughterhouse was somewhat out of the way, at the end of the Promenade Street, although the actual Promenade came to an end a couple of hundred meters away. The slaughterhouse had been built directly over the River for the blood to run into, and often when there had been a lot of slaughtering—at Easter, for example, or at Christmas—the River would run red. The peasants used to say that the Whore was having her period. Or else that the Russians had arrived.

Behind the slaughterhouse was a little hut that had been built as a public convenience. But it was not often people went there merely to relieve themselves. They went because they knew they would find Lolos, the village fool. He supported himself by supplying visitors with paper to wipe themselves, often from some old newspaper.

He saved the sports pages for his best customers. If he could read, the customer took his reading matter and withdrew. Otherwise he would ask Lolos to read aloud while he enjoyed the view out over the River.

Lolos could not read either, but his imagination never failed. He would hold the piece of newspaper at the proper distance from his eyes and, with great earnestness, read aloud about the end of the world, interspersed with remarks about Ialites who did not happen to be present.

This reading aloud cost a little extra, but it was worth the money, for Lolos knew everything about everyone in town. Or so he claimed. He could report on who had seduced who's daughter or sister, who was going to marry whom, he could tell about Hitler's rise to power and about Christos the butcher's lonely nights, which he spent catching flies and committing the sin of Onan.

The butcher hated to squash flies between his fingers. So he had worked out a technique that involved catching a fly in his hand, shaking it vigorously like an unopened bottle of fruit juice, and then throwing it as hard as he could against the wall or the floor. The insect, its brains rattled, could not fly away but simply fell stunned to the floor and the butcher would step on it with his left foot.

Lolos could also tell about the butcher's nights of masturbation. He had seen many men reach orgasm, he claimed, but none of them were a match for the butcher. It flowed like an absolute river, a river of unborn children, as Lolos used to put it. He was convinced that if the butcher got married he could singlehandedly populate all Ialos with his offspring.

Meanwhile the customer sat on his heels, gazed off toward the valley and listened to Lolos' stories. A better cure for constipation did not exist. The Mayor, whose dignity prohibited him from visiting the public outhouse but also endowed him with chronic constipation, used to have Lolos summoned to his presence. The two gentlemen would withdraw, and when they eventually reappeared, joy and relief would be written all over the Mayor's face.

Lolos did not like the Mayor, but he could not deny himself the exquisite opportunity of hearing the most exciting news from the Mayor's own lips. For the Mayor was in the habit of using these privy councils to consult with Lolos on the town's affairs.

"I can't talk to the others, Lolos. They're all scoundrels. Of course you're a fool, but that's not as bad. And then too you don't make a lot of motions and call for votes and all that crap. If I say 'yes' and you say 'no' and I say 'yes' again, then you say 'yes' too. That's the way it's supposed to be."

Little boys often went to the public outhouse, but Lolos would chase them away. He liked children, which was why he didn't think they ought to be there. But the children misunderstood him and hated him. They were also a little scared of him, though not enough to keep them from thinking up a lot of malicious mischief and making fun of the poor man, who was utterly incapable of defending himself against them.

The third shopkeeper—everyone thought of the outhouse as Lolos' shop—had a general store where he sold food and drink, stationery, coffee, hardware, and everything else that a small town might need.

In the cellar he had fixed up a room where he served wine and ouzo to go with the food the peasants brought in with them. Often game, after a good day of hunting. The storekeeper was a genial man with a big belly. He was tremendously popular in the town because he extended credit to everyone and never grumbled.

He knew what he was doing. He not only bound his customers

to him, but when they could not pay cash, which was often the case, he was content to accept payment in farm goods which he then turned around and sold back to them at a higher price.

He was married and had three daughters, and his sorrow at not having a son was profound and well known in the entire region. It was often the subject of discussion at the tavern in the evenings, and there were many who hinted that the storekeeper was still young enough to have a son. But the storekeeper would look at them sadly and reply that indeed he was young enough but that he could no longer make love to his wife.

"It doesn't matter whose ass I grab, hers or my own, it's all the same," was the way he used to conclude his defense. The other customers waited for just that conclusion, for it gave them an excuse to suggest that the storekeeper do like the fastest man in the world, that is, run around a pole and copulate with himself. And if a person got himself pregnant that way, the government, through the Ministry of Sport, had promised to pay him a million drachmas. One million drachmas for the first backside baby.

The customers at the tavern never tired of this joke, which was repeated almost every evening. Nor did the storekeeper. And he never had a son, not with his wife nor by any other means.

His wife was not as old and worn as the storekeeper would have had people believe. In actual fact she was one of the most well-preserved middle-aged women in Ialos, and a good many men admired her, especially since they knew the storekeeper was no longer capable.

She did not have to work in the fields, or toil and drudge like other people's wives, and she had access to various creams and cosmetics. But she never took advantage of her opportunites. She had three daughters to marry off and worried about them day and night.

The daughters were ugly, a curse from God. They were short and fat and dark. But they had pleasing voices that warmed the air as soon as they opened their mouths. Their voices could raise the dead, people used to say, and everyone predicted a brilliant future for them singing at funerals.

There were no longer any funeral singers of note. There was one old woman of eighty-seven who knew all the funeral songs, but she knew all the other songs too, and got them mixed up. In the middle of a funeral she might sing a wedding song or a battle song from the War of Liberation from the Turks in 1821.

It had become very dangerous to employ her, and people complained but thought they could see a solution in the storekeeper's daughters. They really could sing beautifully. And yet you never forgot their ugliness—the singing seemed to emphasize it.

The fourth shop in town was the pharmacy. By "shop" is meant every facility so arranged that there were wares and a counter and at least one person behind this counter who sold these wares without having to go from door to door. For there were otherwise a great many people who bought and sold.

But the pharmacy was a real shop. There were wares and a counter, and behind the counter stood the Pharmacist himself, who in younger years had studied pharmacology in Paris where he wrote a doctoral dissertation on the medicinal value of the dandelion.

The Pharmacist had wanted to stay in Paris, but his father, who was also a pharmacist (at that time called a "quacksalver"), wrote him a short letter. "Come home. Or I will come and get you."

In the face of such a letter there was not much he could do. The old quacksalver was known throughout the province as a man who kept his word, even at the risk of his own or someone else's life.

So the Pharmacist took his doctor's diploma, several suits, a Borsalino and some pornographic postcards and went home. The day he arrived, his father died. There were unmarried sisters in the house, and the Pharmacist was forced to remain. He never left.

He amused himself for quite some time by showing his postcards to the Ialites, but then they were stolen. After that, for lack of anything better to do, he got married. His marriage was a masterpiece of matchmaking.

The best matchmaker in town proposed to a very pretty, very wealthy girl from another village without having asked the Pharmacist's permission. When the girl said yes, the matchmaker came to the Pharmacist and asked him what he thought of the young lady in question. The Pharmacist gave his usual honest answer and said he could "eat up" a girl like that three times a day, whereupon the old woman revealed that the girl was in love with him and told him they could be married the next day if he would agree.

The Pharmacist replied that he wanted to sleep on it. But that night he lay in bed feeling lonely. His sisters were married now, and he was lonely and lustful. He got up to make himself a cup of camomile tea, but before he knew what had happened he found himself outside in the dark on his way to see the matchmaker.

"I want to be married in a week."

The matchmaker, who had played for high stakes and won, controlled herself.

"Then go home and go to bed," she said. "It's not a good idea to get married with a cold." And she pointed to the Pharmacist's legs.

And he realized he had come the whole way without any pants on, only his underwear.

The Pharmacist not only sold salves and tablets. When necessary, he could be both doctor and veterinarian. All things said and done, he was quite a learned man, and he read a great deal. He was often to be seen with a book in his hand, even books in foreign alphabets. His bookcase contained both the lesser and greater Larousse, the Encyclopedia Britannica, and a fine collection of Greek classics.

"We've always been pranksters," he used to say when he read Plato. He would underline the sentence that had occasioned the remark and discuss it later with the Schoolmaster or the Lawyer. These three were the village intellectuals. The Mayor had an education too, but people said of him that he went to the university an ass and came back a mule. The Mayor was aware of his own indifference to learning, and he told Lolos in confidence that "those idiots think you can get something done in this world with books. Bullshit. It's hands and cocks and cunts that rule the world." And Lolos nodded in agreement.

It was clear, in any case, that the Mayor himself was ruled by the items mentioned. When he talked about village affairs or domestic Greek politics or even global matters he would move his fingers like an infant practicing its pincer grip. You got the feeling that the Mayor pinched problems in the rump.

The three scholars regarded the Mayor with understanding condescension, but they rarely dared to get involved in a discussion with him, because in spite of his deficient education he had masses of arguments drawn from his knowledge of the people in the village, from his long experience as their master, and from his family traditions.

His family had been breeding mayors for several generations. And it didn't faze him if you proved that his conclusions did not follow logically from his premises. He would only reply that conclusions weren't a lot of damned eggs that all had to come from the same damned hen—and there was something to be said for that argument.

Behind the Promenade was a small street where all of the town's workshops were gathered—metalsmith, plumber, blacksmith, carpenter, mason, and the other craftsmen. The men in this group were not really merchants, but the Ialites considered them the next best thing.

The sheet-metal shop was now run by the unfortunate metalsmith's son, who had inherited his mother's quick tongue and could say astonishing things. He was very popular. The other craftsmen used to gather in his workshop in the evenings, among the tools and pieces of sheet metal, and listen to his wit.

The blacksmith was the quietest of all the craftsmen. He and the butcher were usually considered a good pair. But they were never close. Except secretly. They were both enclosed by silence. They were both very strong, and where the butcher was red with blood, the smith was black from the coal he used to soften up his iron.

The children used to gather at the blacksmith's and watch him pump air into his hearth and then take a set of long tongs and pull out a piece of iron that he would hammer with rhythmical strokes full of power but also full of tenderness. Yes, tenderness. The smith loved to watch the glowing iron, blazing red, as it reacted to every blow of his great hammer. You could see the tension of restraint in his muscles. His arm did not fall on the iron, it came to the iron—heavily to be sure, and maybe painfully—but it did not fall, it came.

"The secret of hammering is being able to hold the hammer back," he used to say. "The hammer wants to strike, the hammer pulls you with it, so you have to fight it with all your strength!"

The blacksmith had whatever strength it took. His arms were

like the trunks of young trees, and when he raised them up it seemed as if there might be birds' nests in his dark armpits.

Smithing is clearly a trade that has won entrance into the world of myth and legend. The smith makes weapons as well as instruments of torture. Moreover he has to be strong to do such heavy work, and strength often brings loneliness.

The masons, of whom there were three, were also striking individuals. They were recognizable by their hands—there was always mortar under their nails—and by their blond hair. All three were extremely handsome men. They were brothers, and their family had been masons for generations. At the nearby village of St. Michael their grandfather had built a hanging bridge that was as beautiful as the waist of a young girl. When the bridge was finished, people flocked from every direction to see it. One architect even came all the way from the capital to meet and talk to the old stonemason.

"How can you make such a beautiful arch with no concrete and no iron reinforcement?" the architect wondered. And the old man replied that what he had built was nothing compared to the dome of Hagia Sofia in Constantinople. And its builders too had worked without concrete or iron.

"You don't build with the materials, my son, you build with your heart as a foundation and your arms as pillars."

The architect cannot have been satisfied with this reply, but the old stonemason said later that he had answered allegorically on purpose. He wanted their age-old secrets to stay within the family.

His sons were also masons, and the present masons were the sons of one of those sons. The sons of the other brothers had emigrated to the States, taking with them only this secret of building without concrete and iron.

The three mason brothers always stuck together. They took their evening promenade together, they sat at the café together, they played cards together, and only played games that called either for three players or for two, such as twist or thirty-one.

Sitting, standing, or walking, they had the sun on their shoulders, as the old women used to say. A small, silent circle of sunlight that surrounded them. The three brothers were the pride of the village. No wedding, no name day, no christening was celebrated without them. Their bright hair spread warmth and made it easier for the old people to see.

A very old woman who had seen them as babies, sleeping in a row in a dark room, reported that she was forced to set out a pail of water beside their beds because of the risk that the room would catch fire. The glow from their heads had been that strong. But now there was also a glow from the heads of the German soldiers.

## FEAR

The summer of 1941 was unusually warm. The following winter was to be unusually cold. It was a winter that would give new hope of liberation to those peoples who were in the Nazi grip. But that summer the German troops were still advancing on all fronts, and nothing seemed able to stop them. One country after another fell into German hands.

The Jews would soon be exterminated—at least the Jews who happened to be in Europe. But it was not only Jews the Germans were after. Communists were another favorite prey.

In Greece, the prisons had been full of Communists when the war broke out. Many of them managed to escape in the chaos that followed the fall of the Metaxas dictatorship, in spite of its efforts to hold onto such prisoners in order to hand them over to the Germans. The Germans did the same when they left Greece. They turned their congested prisons over to the Security Battalions, that is, to the Greek Fascists.

It was not good to be a Communist during the Second World War. It was almost worse than being a Jew. Jews were being hunted only by the Germans. Everyone was hunting Communists.

The Germans in Ialos were not even looking for Jews, since they knew it was unusual to find them south of Athens. But they were looking for Communists. The German Captain had already questioned the Mayor, and the Mayor had answered that there was only one Communist—the Jew who had managed to flee.

The Captain did not believe him and eventually created his own organization of informers—people who, for a small sum, would deliver him names.

To begin with, the identity of these informers was unknown, but eventually it was obvious who they were. Their motives were not always financial. The feeling of power it gave them, of belonging to the winning side, was often more important than the money.

A great many of these informers did not know themselves what Communism was or what it stood for. But they had a private system for figuring out who was a Communist. There were categories of acts that only Communists committed. People who didn't go to church were Communists. People who didn't believe in God and the King were Communists. People who wanted to abolish the family were Communists. A divorce could be an indication of Communist sympathies. It was only Communists who talked about the need to organize. And so forth.

All it took to be classified as a Communist was to do something that could be associated with such views. Moreover, the informers all had their own personal enemies, and this was an excellent opportunity to get rid of them.

The Germans arrested people indiscriminately and sent them to concentration camps in Germany or to penal labor camps somewhere in Greece. For minor infractions, people were sent to work outside Ialos where for some reason the Germans were building a small airfield.

Eventually there came to be a little group of villagers who were considered Communists. The three masons were among them, the blacksmith (who was the local backgammon master), the postman, the Schoolmaster, the left-hand cantor, the bell ringer, and Lolos the village fool.

But none of them was thought to be a serious case except the mason who had helped David escape. He was sent to Dachau, and was one of the few who returned alive. The others were allowed to stay in Ialos, doing hard labor at the airfield. A lot of other peasants worked there too, but they were paid wages, and many of them were very proud that Ialos was going to have its own airstrip.

They would sit around during their breaks and imagine the amazement of the emigrants the next time they came home and found—an airfield! There would be airplanes, too.

The men assigned to work on the airfield gathered every morning in the village square. They stood quietly and waited, which they would never have done under normal circumstances. By and by a German corporal would arrive with some soldiers and trucks and a couple of huge dogs. The men had to run like crazy to clamber up onto the trucks, which drove them to the work site.

It was then and there, during those morning hours with their eternal running, that the Ialites began to feel humiliated, insulted, and downtrodden. They were working for the Germans, and that was almost as it should be. But this was slavery! There was no reason they should have to run for the trucks every morning and then balance like sway-pole artists while the corporal sat comfortably in the cab and was never satisfied. He screamed at them all the time, and the peasants gave him the nickname Josef Dog. His real name, of course, was simply Josef.

Josef did not know the art of being an Occupier. All he knew how to be was an executioner and a tyrant. People like Josef bore as much of the responsibility for Hitler's losing the war as did the armies and resistance forces of the countries Hitler fought. Josef could not win the peasants over and thought it was sufficient if they feared him. But he forgot that fear is a feeling no one can live with forever. The peasants thought up jokes to ridicule Josef Dog and, with him, the whole Third Reich. And when jokes were no longer enough, they began to think up other things.

The biggest joker was Uncle Stelios. Everyone knew that. Stelios was the father of the Schoolmaster's wife, and he loved her more than anything else on earth. Every afternoon he fled his own house, where his fanatically religious wife ruled the roost, and went to the Schoolmaster's where he would entertain the whole family.

He could tell countless stories from all the different professions he had had, but the funniest were the ones from his career as a gendarme. He used to ride around among the villages capturing peasant thieves, whom he afterward lost on the way to the provincial capital and jail.

There was still no jail in Ialos, and later, when the town rented a cellar from a peasant as a place to keep people under arrest, Uncle Stelios made up a nursery rhyme about it.

Eventually everyone in the village learned this rhyme, and the soccer team used it as a cheer. It went like this:

"No crime without a crook. No crook without a cop. No cop without a jail. No jail without a merchant. Where's the crime?"

Uncle Stelios had come to Ialos from Egypt as a little boy. There had been a terrible epidemic in Alexandria and children were dying like flies, and Stelios' mother, who was a widow and rather wealthy, had given up everything to try and save her son's life.

And the son's life *was* saved, and he grew into a handsome young man with a mustache and went off to seek his fortune in America. But things went badly in the States and he came back and married a girl from a nearby village called Katavothra. The name means "abyss," or "hole in the earth," and the village had been given the name because the River disappeared there and came up again two kilometers away.

Young Stelios explained his decision to marry a girl from Katavothra (the village naturally had an evil reputation) by observing that after all marriage was the worst abyss a person could fall into. And so he married brown-eyed Maria, who proved to have a fanatical nature—devoted, courageous, and unpredictable.

She was much loved by her grandchildren because of the way she laughed. She did not laugh often, and when she did it seemed to be in spite of herself. She would pretend to be very angry and then suddenly start to cough, and this coughing always turned out to be laughter.

She was especially attached to little Minos and kept a close eye on his dealings with Reveka. One day during the afternoon siesta, when the two children were napping in the same bed, she suddenly appeared out of nowhere and snatched aside the sheet that covered them. When she saw that they were fully clothed, she made the sign of the cross and silently thanked God.

She was very fond of Reveka and cared for her as tenderly as she cared for her own grandchildren. But secretly she meant to convert Reveka to Christianity and lent her all her tracts with stories of the saints, the martyrs, and the apocalypse. These booklets so terrified the children that they eventually stopped reading them. On the other hand, they did know what sin was, and how to do it.

Minos' older brother, who was named after his grandfather Stelios, also kept an eye on the two children. He tormented them every way he could think of. He used to take them out riding on a donkey, and when they reached the cemetery he would jump off, kick the donkey as hard as he could in the direction of the gravestones, and scream at the top of his lungs that now the dead were coming out to get them. And he would dance a little dance to disguise his own terror. He really expected the earth to open at any moment and the dead to come wandering out in long rows with open mouths and enormous teeth.

He had probably read the apocalypse too, in his younger days. But the dead never came. Not even the living came. Occasionally someone would come riding by on a donkey, but these adults never interfered. At the very most they might stop for a moment and holler threats and curses of their own at the terrified children, who wept and pleaded for mercy.

Ialos was a hard school for children, and so were most of the other villages around. It is not so strange that the Greeks were among those who survived best in Hitler's concentration camps. When the war was over, statistics showed an amazingly high percentage of Greek survivors.

The person who is born in hell has the best chance of surviving there. In 1941 hell had not yet come to Greece in earnest, but it would not be long. The people were getting tired of seeing their fields plundered by German and Italian soldiers. Famine was not far off. In Athens food was already in short supply. The Black Market had made its appearance and would eventually be the only market there was.

Uncle Stelios, the great joker, couldn't help making up songs about almost everything and wrote the following song about Josef Dog, which the peasants would sing as they worked.

We've got Josef the Dog,
and he eats like a hog
and he sleeps and he shits
and he farts and has fits,
and he screams for more strips
for all Hitler's airships.
Jesus Christ, what a pest!
What we need is a rest!

Josef went pale when he heard the song from one of the informers. He immediately sent for old Stelios and boxed his ears and kicked him, in front of the other peasants. The old man didn't make a move to defend himself. But tears could be seen glistening deep in his eyes.

"He thinks it hurts, the stupid shit," he whispered to the men around him.

And it did hurt, but Stelios stood it. He held himself in check, and the German, meeting no resistance, finally got bored. He blew his whistle and all the men went back to work. Stelios lay still for a moment and then struggled to his feet, picked up his spade and went on with his song, although now he sang it silently to himself. He had already started thinking up a new one. It was going to be about the Gendarmerie Commander and all the other officials who cheerfully saw to it that the town continued to function as it had before the Occupation.

## THE OFFICIALS

The Ialos officials could be divided into two categories—those who had power (or who exercised it) and those who had none.

The Gendarmerie Commander was the representative of power and, by virtue of that fact, had power himself. The Schoolmaster had no power. The Magistrate who came to the village once a month had power. The Priest was somewhere in between—he both did and did not have power. The Lawyer had no real power, but he was close to power.

The Surveyor had power, and so did the man who was in charge of the manure-spreader and the binder. This man should not have had any power, but he borrowed a certain authority from the fact that his mother's brother was a Member of Parliament.

This mechanic was an unpredictable man. No one ever really knew when and where he was going to fertilize. He followed a list drawn up by the county agronomist, but he read the list in a different direction each day. When some farmer complained, he would answer in a superior tone that he went by a government list, which could not be altered. If the farmer insisted and pointed out that according to the list it was his turn, the mechanic would remind him that although the government had indeed made the list, it was the mechanic alone who decided in which order to follow it. No one had ever continued to insist beyond that point because of the risk that the mechanic would spread plant poison instead of fertilizer on the troublemaker's fields.

In fact this had actually occurred. The farmer in question instituted a lawsuit in 1938, but it was postponed several times and no decision was handed down until 1949, when the civil war was over and both the farmer and the mechanic had been dead for years.

The gendarmerie detachment in Ialos consisted of three gendarmes and their commander, who held the rank of lieutenant. The commander was from Crete, as were two of the gendarmes. The third was from a village in the neighborhood. He would never have been allowed to serve so close to his native village if he had not had a connection in some ministry. (In the language of Ialos, this was known as "having teeth.")

The gendarmerie and the army adhered to the principle that as far as possible personnel should not serve near their own home towns. The reason was very simple. They did not want the men to feel any loyalty toward the civilian population. One of the most important elements in the training of gendarmes and soldiers alike was to fill them with hatred and contempt for civilians and civilian institutions.

The Gendarmerie Commander was about fifty years old and had been promoted to lieutenant quite recently. He had come up the hard way, through the ranks. He had begun as a simple gendarme. Then he became lance corporal, then corporal, sergeant, and staff sergeant, and now he had reached the highest possible rank that a man of his education could achieve. Unless there was a war, of course, for a war would create lots of opportunities.

No one in the village would ever forget the day the Commander received his promotion. The men were sitting at the café talking about Sunday's soccer match between the Upper Town and the Lower Town when the postman brought the Commander a brown envelope with a lot of stamps on it.

The Commander, who had obviously been expecting this letter, turned quite red in the face and walked hastily to his office. A few moments later there came a sudden howl from inside, followed by a string of curses and threats—now he'd show the bastards, now there was going to be hell to pay, and so forth.

The Ialites naturally assumed that the letter contained bad news, but in fact it was the notification of his promotion. The Commander came out half an hour later wearing his new epaulets and let everyone present buy him a drink.

"A lieutenant is a lieutenant," he said. "And no one had damned well better forget it!"

And it was true that no one ever forgot to call him Lieutenant after that. Although this was probably because most of them had started calling him Lieutenant long before, merely to flatter him and to soften his Cretan heart.

The Greeks on the mainland have no very high opinion of Crete and its inhabitants. They consider them barbarians, originally from Mongolia. The Cretans, for their part, cherish no particularly warm feelings for the mainland Greeks either. They regard them as stupid, cowardly, and traitorous.

Crete had not had a traitor in two thousand years, they always claimed, and there was some truth to what they said. Informing, which is almost an honorable profession on the mainland, has never become widespread on Crete.

There may be a number of reasons for this, and yet the decisive factor must be that those informers who did occasionally appear on Crete always met an early, brutal death. On the mainland, the situation was almost the reverse. Informers were the only people who ever rose in the social hierarchy.

The two gendarmes from Crete were fiercely loyal to their commander and fellow Cretan. They were unflinchingly obedient and saw to it that the third gendarme danced to the Lieutenant's tune as well. This third gendarme was a somewhat insubordinate young man otherwise, and everyone predicted that he would not last long in the gendarmerie. And they were partly right.

In a little town like Ialos, it was difficult for the representatives of power not to mix with the population. In addition to which, their unpretentious salaries forced them to turn to the people for various services that the peasants performed free of charge in order to keep themselves on a good footing with the authorities. They also had to get the peasants to treat them to retsina or ouzo at the tavern, for otherwise their salaries could only be stretched far enough for an ordinary Saturday-night drunk.

For their part, the peasants handled these relationships with finesse and sensitivity. They exploited their opportunities, but not to excess. They would lose one or two games of twist to the gendarmes, but never more.

Backgammon was very popular in Ialos, and it was a great honor to be a good player. For some reason, card games were thought to involve more luck than backgammon. In actual fact they both depended equally on luck, although of course a person did need a certain skill to make the best of good cards or a lucky throw of the dice. But whereas it was considered impossible to affect the cards, everyone believed the dice could be influenced by a variety of magic spells and tricks.

In the first place, they had to be shaken in the proper manner. One of the Cretan gendarmes had it down to an art. He closed his hand loosely around the dice, leaving a gap between forefinger and thumb—exactly the way a man holds his penis when he masturbates. Then he rolled his hand back and forth from the wrist, gently to begin with, then gradually increasing the tempo until the dice flew out in a kind of backgammon ejaculation.

This gendarme knew no master at the game. The only man who could even compete with him was the quiet blacksmith. In contrast to everyone else, the blacksmith played without either damning his luck or thanking his lucky stars, without slamming the flat of his hand on the table and without glowering at the people around him.

But all the racket he did not make himself was made for him by his supporters. The smith's duels with the gendarme were well attended. People sat or stood around the table and followed the progress of the game anxiously but not quietly. The Lieutenant and the second gendarme sat behind their player, while the third gendarme, who didn't really want to show his feelings, never watched.

These matches were seen as a battle between Crete and the southern Peloponnesus. If the blacksmith won, there was a party at the café. The peasants would buy drinks for everyone and were even more generous than usual. For this reason, the Cretan gendarme had been ordered by his commander to let the smith win now and then.

"A good player has to be able to lose too," the Lieutenant said, thereby implying that when he himself lost it was deliberate.

The Magistrate who traveled around among these villages did not, obviously, have much contact with the local populace. He stayed either at the Lawyer's or at the Mayor's, because there was not yet any hotel in Ialos, though one would soon be built.

The Magistrate looked very strict and appeared to suffer from a chronic ulcer, but he had gentle eyes which he hid behind glasses.

He was the son of a poor peasant from a little village in the mountains on the other side of Sparta. His family had made fantastic sacrifices to enable him to attend the university, and now he made sacrifices for his four unmarried sisters.

He never married. His sisters were no longer young, and there was virtually no hope that they would ever marry. The Magistrate toiled and saved to give them proper dowries, but his salary was simply insufficient.

He lived in the provincial capital and could be seen in the evenings with his sisters, partaking of a so-called "U-boat"—hot vanilla dropped into cold water. He was not allowed to drink ouzo or coffee because of his bad stomach. His sisters tried every way they could think of to cheer themselves up—they laughed a lot, and instead of walking normally they would trip down the street like four hens.

But getting married was beyond them. In the end they resigned themselves and concentrated their frustrated tenderness on their brother, who was moreover the youngest of the five. He had to dress the way they wanted him to, he had to eat the food they thought he ought to have, he had to go around wearing a ridiculous wool scarf when the temperature was seventy degrees.

But the Magistrate endured it. No one could understand how. The secret was that the Magistrate wrote poetry. Even when he sat in court listening to a case he was writing poetry. Or rather then in particular, for it was then he felt most lonely.

People quarreled and fought and killed each other for so little—a tree growing right on the boundary between two fields, a goat eating someone's grapevines. He found it hard to believe that these people were really only concerned about the material damage. He suspected other motives behind these feuds, but he did not know what they were.

The Magistrate also collected the folk songs he heard on his travels. He had a great love for the poetry that "this poor people" had created. Some day, after his retirement, he would publish his poems and his collection of folk songs.

"I have not created harmony. The least I can do is shed light on the causes of discord," he would mutter to himself.

He was not the only one with such thoughts. There had been so many wars and so much suffering, that no one still believed a reasonable life was possible. The Magistrate was a devout democrat. Nevertheless, only twice in his whole career had he served a democratic government. He had often thought of quitting, often dreamed of it at night, but then he always saw the accusing faces of his four sisters—four pairs of black eyes, and without a tear, or a word, the eyes would widen to make room for pain and he would leap out of bed with his heart in his throat.

After all, dying a magistrate was not the worst fate in the world. When he came to Ialos he usually stayed with the Lawyer. He should not have done so, actually. His place was at the Mayor's. But he did not like the Mayor's. The Mayor was a generous host, but his generosity sometimes felt insulting and brutal. Moreover, the Mayor's diet was much too heavy for a man with an ulcer.

The Magistrate preferred the Lawyer, a more peaceable man who had chosen the wrong profession. No peaceable lawyer has any chance of succeeding in Greece. Lawyers are to the Greeks what toreadors are to the Spanish. They must somehow make themselves legendary or they never get any clients.

But because the law was such a glamorous profession, many young men chose it without having the necessary qualifications for success—nerve, a big mouth, a good (rich) family behind them, contempt for the law, good contacts with judges, and so forth.

As a result, many of these young men never got any further than the stairwells outside the great courtrooms. They walked around and whispered to each other and took off their hats whenever a famous lawyer passed, for they respected the men who had succeeded, even though they knew that most of them were asses. But an ass who succeeds is no longer an ass. Success makes him a thoroughbred.

The lawyer in Ialos, Sotirios Kostaváras, was a mediocre lawyer. He had tried to make a career for himself in the capital, but he never got further than insignificant petty thefts and fist fights. The big murder cases never materialized, and he found himself forced to return to the village. He hadn't liked the city anyway—people everywhere, shouting and screaming, bustle, dust, bad water, and hordes of swindlers.

Thefts and fights were not as common in the village as they had been in the city, but here he could be alone. He had no competitors to slander him and stab him in the back. Had he stayed in the city he would undoubtedly have wound up in the lowest category of his profession, that is to say, among those lawyers who took their fees not in hard cash but in kind: eggs, salamis, bread, cheese, olives, and the like. These lawyers had not seen the inside of a courtroom since their student days. They mostly wrote petitions to different governmental agencies on behalf of peasant clients. They ranked socially just above con men and sharpers.

The Lawyer and the Magistrate had failed for a reason that brings failure only in Greece: they were both a little too honest. In the evenings they would sit in the Lawyer's spacious parlor with its fireplace and go over the cases they were to take up the next day. Objectively and soberly they discussed the evidence and the punishment that should be meted out to each guilty party, and the next morning they went to the courtroom and acted out their roles before arriving at the predetermined verdict.

Both of them were capable of flaming up, and then the words would fall from their mouths in torrents warm with a longing for justice and wisdom. The peasants would watch in astonishment. Where did all the words come from? How could so much blood rush to the cheeks of the exhausted Magistrate? How could this timid Lawyer be transformed into a lion?

The peasants came to the conclusion that being a lawyer or a judge was a talent you had to be born with. After the battle, the two warriors would withdraw, drink each other's health—the Magistrate stuck to watered wine—eat a good dinner, and the Circuit Magistrate would travel on.

These hours in the courtroom nourished them for weeks—until it was time for the next performance. When the Magistrate had gone, the Lawyer went back to the Schoolmaster and the Pharmacist, and they talked as usual of religion, crime, and the people.

## RELIGION

The Greek people have always had problems with their kings, presidents, generals, and bishops. Their gods, on the other hand, have never given them much trouble. It is true that Zeus came down to earth in the old days and carried off an occasional pretty girl, whom he invariably knocked up, but in general he used his lightning very sensibly.

When paganism was replaced by Christianity—and this was accomplished with force and violence, in case anyone thought otherwise—the Greek people maintained contact with their earlier religion by carrying over a number of melodies, ceremonies, and customs.

The church never became a place people went to alone in order to commune with God. The church retained the social function it had had in pagan times. It became Christianity's *agora*. It was in church you met your friends, took a good look at their wives and daughters, and conducted business. In addition, churches were surrounded by cafés, not by churchyards as in other countries.

After receiving Christ's body and blood, a person washed it down with several glasses of ouzo or retsina. This might be considered a weakness in the church but was actually its strength. Not to take part in the life of the church was like not taking part in the life of society, and nothing scared an Ialite more than the possibility of being thought a recluse.

The Ialites had mastered the art of paying homage to individualism and conformity at the same time. Every man was a world unto himself, of course, but all worlds were alike, and woe to him who did not want to be or who actually was not like everyone else.

Conflicts between the townspeople were often dealt with by the Priest or some other man of the church. But not all types of conflicts. Only those of a moral nature. That is to say, those that were not covered in the law books. For as soon as a thing was mentioned in the law, the Priest's authority ceased and a lawyer had to be called in.

The Ialites loved lawsuits. But not everyone could afford them. To litigate was a step upward and allowed a man to sit at his café in the evenings and tell everyone about all the clever tricks his lawyer had thought up.

Or he could say, "Yes, tomorrow I have to go in to the city again. I've got to clear up that lawsuit, you know." And whoever he was talking to *did* know and was absolutely green with envy.

The man who carried the art of litigation furthest was a relatively well-to-do farmer who quickly managed to ruin himself. All of his money and possessions went to lawyers. People called him Procedure, because for some reason he loved this word and used it whenever he could and often when he could not.

He brought suits against all sorts of people for all sorts of reasons. His eyes were constantly swollen from lack of sleep, for he stayed awake at night trying to discover all the injuries he supposed people had committed against him.

His wife and children begged him with tears in their eyes to do his work and see to the crops and the livestock, but he had been burned by the sun of justice. He sued everything that moved. The lawyers fleeced him thoroughly and he fell into poverty and finally had to conduct his suits without legal assistance, which of course meant an end to justice.

Procedure met a grandiose fate. His wife declared him insane. He brightened up immediately and brought suit against her, and then everyone realized that he really was sick and they carried him off to the Daphne Madhouse outside Athens.

From there he dispatched masses of petitions and applications to all sorts of ministries and departments. Shortly before he died he sent a message to the Mayor reading, "Justice shall triumph in the end."

It gave the Mayor a good laugh. "Ho ho!" he said. "Only Procedure would think of a crazy thing like that."

People also went to church to be seen. They put on their best clothes, combed their hair, washed their faces, shaved, and every Sunday hoped the congregation would be struck with amazement when they made their appearance.

But the congregation was never struck with amazement, since every member of it expected amazement from the others. The only person who ever managed to raise eyebrows was an emigrant who after twenty years in the States was still not free of his need to impress his countrymen.

He went to church in an American Indian costume, and when the Priest came out to the altar and caught sight of the emigrant he was absolutely beside himself. He made the sign of the cross and said loudly, "Is it true what my eyes tell me, or is this some invention of the devil?"

The right-hand cantor responded as if in a Byzantine hymn. "It is absolutely true, most reverend sir. This devil is pulling our leg!"

The Priest wanted to have the man thrown out, but the congregation took his side. A person had a right to come to God exactly as he wanted. There was a brief trial in the middle of mass, and in the end the Priest gave in. For once, individualism won.

The Ialites believed in God. But they used their faith shrewdly, the same way they used everything else. There were exceptions of course—atheists and fanatics—but they were rare. The Ialites were forced to spend their whole lives bent over the soil, and when they turned their eyes to heaven it was to look at the weather, not to pray to God.

## THE CRIMINALS

The town had no criminals in the usual sense of the word. Assault, petty theft, and fraud did occur, but these crimes were not considered very serious, and those who committed them were accepted back into the community after taking their punishment. So there were lawbreakers but no real felons.

Moreover, most people admired a successful swindler. Cheating people out of their money and possessions was considered a notable achievement. The Ialites hated to be cheated. To allow yourself to be swindled was to declare yourself an incompetent and an idiot.

Long stories about someone cheating someone else were constantly told at the cafés and never failed to provoke great hilarity among the listeners.

"What a fox!" they all said.

The fox was thought to be cunning, and there was practically a celebration whenever a fox was spotted on the slopes of One Arm. The whole town would set off—not to kill the fox exactly, but to smoke him out. They wanted to show the fox he wasn't worth much compared to descendants of the ancient Spartans.

They would beat the slopes and chase the fox into a cave. Then they would light a fire in front of the entrance. The beautiful animal would be afraid to come out but could not stay in the cave, either, because of the smoke. The fox would howl in desperation, but when the flames drew close it finally had to rush through them. The leap through the flames always set fire to some of the animal's coat, and the peasants would run after this living torch and holler and scream and shout jokes and taunts and make fun of the fox's plight.

Most of the foxes got away. They would jump into the River and put the fire out. But no fox with a singed pelt ever showed itself in the vicinity of Ialos again.

"They're embarrassed," the peasants believed. "We outfoxed them." Craftiness was a virtue, but only if successful. Tricksters were appreciated even in ancient Greece. Of all the famous boxers and wrestlers, the most famous was the one who invented tripping. In Sparta, stealing was not thought very serious as long as a person wasn't caught. The trick Ulysses played on the Trojans was preserved for humanity by the blind poet Homer, who was not blind for nothing.

In Ialos, consequently, criminality of a certain kind was approved and accepted. But there were exceptions. When the hanged confectioner's sons set fire to a barn, and two horses, a donkey, and several sheep and goats were reduced to smoke and ashes, people felt the two of them should be arrested and sent to the prison in Palamidi, where the cruelest murderers were kept, along with political prisoners.

Palamidi Prison was infamous, partly because almost no one had ever come out of it alive, and partly because many of the men who carried out and won the revolt against the Turks in 1821 wound up there.

Those men were the first political prisoners in modern Greek history, and Palamidi was to receive many more in the years that followed. The prison stood on a small peninsula outside the city of Navplion in the Peloponnesus. Navplion became the first capital of the newly formed Greek state in 1827. The first president, Kapodistrias, was murdered in Navplion, and the bullet hole can still be seen in the wall of a building in the center of the city.

Kapodistrias had also sent people to Palamidi. Many of the cells were underground and knee-deep in water. There was a little hole through which the prisoners could see the sky, and any number of their songs were about this blue Greek sky that has always filled the hearts of all true Greeks with incomprehensible pride. In fact, of course, the Greeks have not made their own sky any more than other peoples have made theirs. But even the ancient Athenians bragged about the fine air and the harmonious landscape of Attica.

It would seem that the Greeks have a great need to boast. In fact the language contains words meaning "brag" or "boast" that are used as words of love.

*Kamari mou* can be said to a child or a lover. What it means is actually "you who make me so proud." Or *kamaromouna,* which refers to a proud vagina, whatever that may be.

By the same mysterious logic, people could also boast about Palamidi Prison. And it was not only the people who did so. Prime Minister Kanellopoulos, who once wrote a thick tome on European intellectual history, wanted to call Makronisos—a dreaded island prison where Communists were "re-educated" by means of a variety of tortures—"The New Parthenon."

In any case, the confectioner's two boys were sent to Palamidi Prison. They had both been found guilty, and also stood accused of being Communists. Their very crime, arson, was considered adequate proof of their ideological leanings. Because only Communists did such things.

The Greek Communist Party was founded in 1918, and ever since, its members, or those thought to be members or sympathizers, have been hunted, persecuted, put in prison, and sent into exile.

So Ialos had no criminals in the usual sense of the word, but it did have two Communists. The boys' alleged Communism was nonexistent, of course. They hardly knew the meaning of the word. They were terribly ashamed of being put into prison as Communists. There were a lot of people in Greece at that time who would have been mortified if anyone had thought they were Communists.

General Metaxas, who seized power in a coup on August 4, 1936, began a war of extermination against the Communists. Aided by his Minister of the Interior, Maniadakis, he put most of the important leaders into prison or onto exile islands, prohibited the Party newspaper, and introduced a system for certifying every citizen's political dependability.

General Metaxas wanted to force on Greece a system resembling Mussolini's, but King George II, who was pro-British, exerted political pressure and Metaxas began to vacillate between two policies. But soon he had to take a stand. On October 26, 1940, Mussolini demanded a Greek capitulation. Metaxas answered "no," against his will, and this "no" has transformed a dictator into a hero. The truth was simply that Metaxas did not dare take the risk of opposing the King.

The Italian army attacked Greece on October 28, but the war went badly for the Italians. They suffered heavy casualties and lost a number of battles. When, in April 1941, the Germans stepped in, the Italians were on the retreat.

The hanged confectioner's boys were the only people from Ialos who had ever been in Palamidi. They were also among the few who ever came out. They would return to the village with new songs and a bird they had tamed while in prison. A swallow.

## THE PEOPLE

The people of Ialos were primarily peasants. Some of them had a piece of land, others did not. Those who had only a little land could hardly make ends meet on that alone. They also had to work for Mousouris, or raise a few pigs and goats. But even then these peasants were more fortunate than those who had no land at all.

The latter were completely dependent on Mousouris and, what was worse, on the government projects that occasionally cropped up. Roads mostly. All dictators love to build roads and monuments. Not because they possess any secret architectural aptitude, like Hitler, but because this is the easiest way for them to create employment and gain control of the populace.

For a real farmer, there is nothing worse than being a hired laborer. The peasants were ashamed of having to gather in the square every morning to be carted to work in a military vehicle. The peasants were used to waking up whenever they wanted to; they were used to taking a break in their work whenever they themselves decided. They were not used to dancing to someone else's tune like a gypsy bear.

The dictatorship in Athens believed it could win the people to its cause by offering them employment. It did not take into account the virtue—or vice—which the Ialites called *filotimo* and which meant that a man loved his honor above all else. Many murders are committed in Greece every year for reasons having to do with the murderer's honor. A farmer's honor forbids him to work as a hired hand.

Naturally some people were fooled and fell for the dictator's scheme. New roads were always a good thing to have. A person might have to rush to the doctor. The mail and the papers would arrive more quickly. But in actual fact the new roads brought only the Germans. This made people wonder if the roads had been built with the Germans in mind.

And they probably had. At least in part. General Metaxas had Fascist ideals himself. He had no reason to fight the Fascists and the Nazis. When Mussolini declared war on Greece, the interned Communists sent a letter to the regime begging to be enrolled in the army. The General Secretary of the Communist Party, Zachariadis, wrote an open letter from prison which the newspapers printed. Zachariadis went so far as to support Metaxas' war, in order to make the Greek Communists realize that the most important thing at that moment was the fight against Facist imperialism. They could deal with Metaxas later.

But Metaxas replied through his Minister of the Interior, Maniadakis, that he was at war with Italy, not with Fascism. So the Communists had to stay in their prisons and on their exile islands. Although many, indeed most of them managed to escape in spite of an increase in the number of guards.

Communism had been thoroughly disparaged. With the exception of a few areas in northern Greece, the Greek countryside was predominantly anti-Communist. Not until after the resistance war against the Germans would the Communists win a place in the hearts of the people.

In Ialos, anti-Communist feeling was and still is very strong. The entire region is among the most reactionary in all of Greece. The only parties that could hope for any votes were those on the far right. But since the parties often changed names, the people preferred to follow a right-wing leader, regardless of which combination of parties he was involved with at the moment.

In one of the few elections in which the Greek Communist Party (KKE) took part, it received one vote from Ialos. Even that caused a great scandal. People scratched their heads, wondering who among them was the traitor. That was 1926. Altogether, KKE won 10 delegates out of 286, all 10 of them from districts in northern Greece.

Two of these delegates were Greek Jews from Thessalonica: Jack Ventura and David Behar Solan. So everyone in Ialos believed that it was David Kalin who had voted for the Communists. It is possible that Kalin was a Communist. But he was definitely not the man who gave the Communists that one vote. Later, much later, it was discovered that the Schoolmaster was the one who had done it.

The Greek Communist Party made a mistake at an early stage that it would suffer for right up into the 1970s. During the Balkan Wars, the Communists flouted the national ego by opposing the occupation of the territories of the Macedonian minority.

This position, which in the historical perspective was both correct and truly socialist, cost the Communists a heavy price. Bourgeois propaganda accused them of treason. They were called Bulgarians. It was said that they wanted to sell the Acropolis to Bulgaria, that they wanted to burn the churches, dissolve the family, and much more.

People believed this propaganda because they also believed that Greece should occupy Macedonia. The people have never willingly denied themselves new territory. No one knew of the privations and sufferings that the Macedonians were forced to endure. The people did not know that General Metaxas had given an order that every Macedonian who used his own language instead of Greek was to have a dose of castor oil forced down his throat, nor that the Macedonians lived in profound poverty, nor that their children suffered a terrible death rate, nor, finally, that the Macedonians were an independent people with their own culture and history. But then the Greeks have always underestimated their neighbors.

The people of Ialos saw Communism as a disease and a betrayal. They did not want to know more than that. They were not exactly in favor of the dictatorship, it was simply that they had no interest in ideological questions. As long as they could keep their land and their animals, that was all that mattered. Who was in power made little or no difference.

The Ialites did not care about politics in the strict sense. They might quarrel about who should be the new mayor, but whether or not Greece should enter into an alliance with the Fascists was a question that only a few people bothered their heads about. The Greek people have a long political tradition, but it is only a micropolitical tradition. A power struggle among acquaintances.

The occasional Greek politicians who have risen above this sort of power struggle have, since ancient times, died in exile, prison, or the torture chamber. From Aristides and Themistocles to Passalides, chairman of the EDA party.

So much intelligence has been killed in Greece that the Greeks might well hang their heads in shame forever. But Greeks have a hard time feeling shame for what they do themselves. On the other hand they are very readily ashamed of what other people force them to do.

# *Part III*

# THE HARD YEARS

# THE AVENGERS

At the end of July, the hanged confectioner's two boys came back to Ialos from Palamidi Prison. They had been gone since 1939, victims of a regime that had made the elimination of Communism its principal program.

When their father committed suicide, the two boys were twelve and thirteen years old. But not even death could save the confectioner's honor. While he lived he was a living faggot, and after his death he was a dead faggot, but still a faggot.

The Ialites went around telling the wildest stories about the confectioner. How he'd been caught in the act with a man from another village. How for lack of anything better he had tried to get himself fucked by a dog. How he had fondled little boys.

None of it was true, and no one had seen a thing. There had been rumors even when the confectioner was a child. What *was* true was that as a boy the confectioner had had an unusually gentle voice, which made him a great success with the girls. But even that was turned to his disadvantage and said to depend not on his masculinity but rather on its absence. Birds of a feather, as the saying went.

It took a long time for the confectioner—who was not yet then a confectioner—to become aware of his reputation. And then he begged his mother, Maria, with death at her heels, to let him move away. He wanted to go to Athens. But when Maria, in her desperation, mentioned this to some of the neighboring wives, they implied that they knew why he wanted to move far away from Ialos.

The old woman realized immediately what sorts of rumors were being spread and grew even more desperate. She begged and pleaded with her son to stay in Ialos, to get married and have children as quickly as he could. When he objected that he was still too young to get married, she did not dare tell him what she knew but set up a smokescreen instead about how old she was and how she didn't want to die before her hands had held a grandchild.

This wish seemed legitimate and easy to understand, and even the confectioner realized that the Ialites would use his departure to break the old woman's heart. So he stayed. But he had no job. He could not be a farmer, because once a man was suspected of homosexuality he could not work for men or among men. For the same reason he also escaped the draft.

Now both the mother and the son were desperate, and the mother lay awake at night and thought about taking a gun and doing what the metalsmith's wife had done. Or maybe she should put the gun in her son's hands and say to him, "Off with you. And when you come back, if you do, do not come back with wounds. And if you do have wounds, let them be on your breast, not your back. Now go off and save your name, and the name of your blessed father, God forgive him."

But the old woman could not bear to think of her son's death. Moreover, she noticed that deep down she too had begun to doubt his masculinity. She fell victim to that logic which is the rumormonger's strongest weapon: "How else could the rumor have started? Where there's smoke, there's fire."

The old woman and her son finally arrived at a compromise, but it was a compromise reached in panic, and they did not think through its consequences. In an unfortunate moment they agreed that the son should go to Patra, a relatively large city on the west coast of the Peloponnesus, and there he would study the art of pastry baking and learn how to make vanilla and a special kind of candy found only in the Balkans.

This candy is called *loukoumi* and is made of a kind of jelly coated with fine sugar. It is every child's delight, but unhappily for the confectioner and his mother, loukoumi is considered to be to the homosexual what the apple was to Adam.

If a man had the slightest tendency in that direction and began to eat loukoumi or, worse yet, to make it, then he was doomed to end his days on some back street in Athens, lying in wait for soldiers and sailors and waving a few trembling bills in their faces in hopes of attracting a temporary stud.

To make matters worse, the whole city of Patra, which was famous for its loukoumi, was regarded as a hotbed of homosexuality, and every decent Greek knew that a faggot was always a faggot but a faggot from Patra was a faggot twice over.

When the young man came back to Ialos after his sojourn in Patra he had still never slept with either a man or a woman. Unfortunately, the Ialites already regarded his homosexuality as a proven fact. People went to the little bakery he opened, for he did make excellent pastries, but when they came in they would first give the confectioner a long, knowing look and then order their loukoumi, or some other sweet, in a voice filled with innuendo.

Nevertheless, the confectioner married and had two sons. But the rumors continued; they merely changed tenor. His wife was suspected of infidelity. Various men were mentioned as possible fathers of the children, among them the Mayor. He denied the rumors but not very energetically, since the confectioner's wife was very "edible" and came from another village so that the Mayor did not have to fear any objections from her family.

Life became very difficult for the couple. The confectioner could not show himself on the street without someone coming up and asking him innocently how loukoumi was made or how much it cost, and people questioned the two little boys about the family's habits, and someone wrote on the wall of their house LOUKOUMI AND OTHER GOODIES FOR SALE HERE. But the confectioner and his wife endured it all.

When the Ialites finally realized that they couldn't get to the confectioner with rumors, they began discussing his homosexuality openly. They complained to the Mayor and the Priest. They were afraid he would seduce their sons, for quite recently someone who didn't want his name mentioned had seen the confectioner fondling a little boy behind the counter, and maybe the boy was little but he did have a cock, and the person who did not want his name mentioned had seen it and was amazed.

Children grew up quickly these days. Moreover the whole town smelled of sodomy because the confectioner manufactured his own loukoumi, and it was not long before people couldn't show their faces in another village without being asked if anyone else in Ialos had started making that delicious loukoumi. It got to be a question of Ialos' honor and good name. They could not tolerate a faggot in their midst forever. They considered collecting names on a petition to send to the provincial capital and they asked the Mayor about it, but he waved the idea aside.

"The authorities have more than enough to do with all the Communists," he said. "Christ, if they've got to keep a check on every faggot's asshole, too, why we'll have to import cops from Turkey!"

The Turks were considered very adept at detecting faggots. The Mayor proposed instead that they report the confectioner for child molestation. But no one in Ialos would make the report, or at least no one would sign it.

So the Mayor suggested they leave the whole thing to him. There was very little he had to do. The confectioner was worn out. Hell had come to him, and he had lived in hell for many years, but at last he couldn't go on.

He wrote a short message to his wife and kissed his two boys, and later they found him dangling in the chestnut tree. And even then someone remarked on how faggots apparently had to have themselves a little number even right at the very last. It was a well-known fact that hanging produced an ejaculation.

The confectioner's wife stayed in Ialos. She kept very much to herself for several months and never went out. The little bakery-café was closed down, and destitution was imminent when she suddenly realized she had to make a final effort for the children's sake. She dried her tears, washed her face, hung her husband's key ring at her waist, and went to the bakery, which has not been closed since except on election days, and those are not frequent.

This beautiful, lonely woman became a great challenge to the town's male population. They followed her everywhere. They annoyed her without any regard for her feelings or the feelings of her children. She needed to remarry, but there was no one she wanted to get married to, and no one who could imagine marrying her.

But she required a man in the house. For, as the song says, "A family without a man is like a house without a roof." And even a leaky roof was better than none. The confectioner's wife chose the only possible solution. She took a secret lover. He did not remain secret for very long, but now at least she had a shoulder to rest on at night when she began to tremble at the memory of her husband's body dangling in the tree. Her lover was the Gendarmerie Commander. He could protect her.

The Gendarmerie Commander, Lieutenant Kiriakos Halakis, thought of the affair in the beginning as an "extra assignment in the service of love," as he put it. But after a while he melted mustaches and all into the lonely woman's embrace and wanted to marry her, but she didn't dare. The children were big now, and she wanted them to honor their father's memory. As a result, the Lieutenant had to sneak into her room late at night, and on his way to these trysts he discovered occasional criminals, whereas otherwise he would never have discovered anything at all.

But the children did not need her sacrifice in order to honor their father's memory. They had seen him hanging there between the foliage and the ground; they had seen his body moving in the short gusts of the morning breeze, and the picture would etch itself into their hearts. That vision would lead them into lives of disgust, terror, and despair.

They were soon told why their father had taken his own life, and they soon learned about the Lieutenant's nightly visits. One night they managed to overcome their drowsiness and stay awake until he arrived.

By and by they heard from their mother's room all the same sounds they had heard when their father was still alive. But these sounds were no longer the sleepy, comforting perceptions of childhood—now they were something quite different. Now they were the sounds of a father betrayed, a mother soiled, and a strange man who would go to his café the next day and boast.

The boys lay absolutely still and held each other's hands. They waited until all the sounds had stopped. Then they crept into the bedroom. Their mother and the Lieutenant were asleep on the bed, naked. He lay with his head on her stomach. There was sweat on his face and he was biting his upper lip as if he were afraid that his soul would leave him in his sleep.

The boys stared at them for a long time. They saw their mother's body, and between her legs they saw white spots—the Lieutenant's sperm drying like fish in the sun. They saw where his rough beard had scratched her breasts.

They saw the Lieutenant's body, the curly hair on his testicles and his buttocks and his chest. One of the brothers suddenly sobbed, and the other began to vomit. They rushed out of the room, their whole bodies trembling. They had seen something dreadful, they believed. In fact they had seen something beautiful, but they had seen it with the eyes of Ialos, like a monk inspecting his scrotum every morning to see if it is still full of worms.

Since that day no one had ever seen them laugh. They always stuck together, and if anyone dared to taunt them they grew violent. They were big, strong boys, and all they had was each other and their despair. It was very hard to reach them. As the years went by, the two boys became the terror of the village.

There were only two adults who had won their hearts—the Schoolmaster and the blacksmith. These were the only two people the boys ever visited between their raids. They vandalized the churches, they beat up other children, they chased the peasants' livestock, and in the evenings they always went to the graveyard where their father had been buried. There had been a lot of difficulty about the burial, since suicide was a serious sin and suicides were not usually buried in hallowed ground.

In the end there had been a compromise. The confectioner was permitted to rest in the ground where he was born, but without a ceremony and without a stone or a cross or any other marker. But after a time someone went to the confectioner's resting place—for it couldn't be called a grave—and left a box of loukoumi.

The boys had seen it and had promised themselves that as soon as they found out who had put it there they would stuff a hundred pieces of loukoumi up his ass and let the flies eat them one by one.

But they never got a chance to redeem this pledge, for it was never determined who the guilty party was. Certain rumors pointed to Lolos, but no one took them seriously. Lolos might be a fool, but he had great respect for the dead.

The boys' childhood had come to a sudden end because of three bodies in three human positions. They had loved their father, and they had despised him for taking his own life and for leaving them. They had loved their mother and despised her too.

Childhood ends where contempt begins. And contempt leads sooner or later to a prison.

It was not long before these two boys became the first teenagers ever to step aboard the military vessel that carried prisoners to Palamidi. They were stuffed into a cell with some men who really were Communists.

In the beginning, the boys closed themselves off. They sat under the little opening in the wall of the cell and stared at the sky and perhaps made plans for their revenge. But after a time, when the days were all alike and the nights were much too lonely, the boys began to respond to the other prisoners. They began to speak when they were spoken to, and after a few more days they were taking part in the prisoners' routine.

They read Marxist pamphlets together, which could always be smuggled in; they discussed the war, and later the Occupation as well; and they planned for the future. Some of the best Communist leaders Greece has ever had were in Palamidi Prison at that time. Men who were wise and self-sacrificing, men who found not a ready-made party they could make a career in, or through, but a party they had to build from scratch. Men who had had to go out and struggle against misinformation and hostility.

Most of those men were killed either by the Germans or else by the Greeks during and after the Civil War. A few of them escaped and live today in Eastern Europe or the Soviet Union.

When the confectioner's boys lost their freedom, their mother lost her lover. Obviously the Gendarmerie Commander could not have a mistress whose sons were considered Communists. The confectioner's widow was alone again, and now there was nothing to keep the peasants from setting their children on her. They pursued her wherever she went, shouting "Commie whore! Commie whore!" behind her back. The Lieutenant writhed in pain, but there was nothing he dared do.

It was clear that the poor woman could not stay in the village unprotected. One night she packed up a few things and walked to a harbor, where she got a place on a small cargo boat headed for Navplion. The crew tried to sleep with her, of course, but the captain knew her family and made them leave her alone.

When she reached Navplion she applied for permission to visit her sons. She had to run up and down a lot of stairs and in and out of a lot of offices before her request was granted.

And then she climbed the whole nine hundred steps that led to Palamidi Prison. With every step she came closer to heaven and closer to her children and closer to the earth. For she was not strong enough. Her eyes turned black and her heart stopped beating and she fell down all nine hundred steps and reached the bottom looking like a piece of ground meat.

One of the guards described what he had seen with the words, "We scooped up the pieces with a teaspoon!"

The brothers were not surprised at this description. They were accustomed to the Greeks' special way of using brutality to relieve their pain and fear. By making a situation worse than it really was, they broke its hold on their emotions. It became a kind of bad dream that they could scoff at and fend off.

The guard did not mean to be unfeeling. He was quite simply shaken, and in order to get a grip on himself he made use of an everyday image, an image a person might even associate with happy mornings, waking up with a cup of hot tea by his bed and the sound of his mother's footsteps in the kitchen, those pattering steps that spread like a carpet of security all through the house.

The brothers asked no more questions. They were granted permission to attend their mother's funeral, but they refused to go. The confectioner's widow had been born in a village on the coast, was married and bore her children inland, and died at the fortress where her sons were imprisoned. She was buried in Navplion and that was an uncommon fate, for few Greek women were not buried in their own villages or cities.

The people of Ialos continued to talk about her for a long time, and she eventually came to be called "the poor fugitive," the Ialites having completely forgotten that it was they who drove her out. They blamed it all on the fact that she had gone off on a long journey all alone, which was asking for trouble.

The brothers' fellow prisoners took them to task for not attending their mother's funeral.

"A good Communist never forgets his mother. After all it's partly for her that he fights."

The brothers answered that they had no intention of forgetting their mother. In that case, the other prisoners wondered, why had they left her alone on her last journey. And the brothers said, "We didn't want to be forgiven. We owed her that!"

The other prisoners didn't really understand, but the brothers gave no further explanation. For that matter, no one asked any further questions, because the brothers had earned a certain respect—the respect always given despair when it is held in check. Because unexpressed despair becomes like a fever, a gleam in the eye, a loneliness that can't be broken through—and people misunderstand and assume they are looking at courage.

It often happens that when people break through the solitude surrounding such individuals they think they have won a victory over the shyness that characterizes all truly courageous men, while what they have really broken through is the isolation enveloping despair.

All revolutionary parties derive their initial strength from just such individuals. But after a while when a more restrained course of action is called for, these individuals become a danger to their comrades and, above all, a danger to the party's goals. A desperate man who has had the joy of forgetting his despair in furious action will be very reluctant to give up such deeds when they are no longer necessary or desirable.

These two brothers, who were to play a prominent role in the mass escape from Palamidi Prison and who were later to become skillful leaders of the first resistance operations, these two brothers would ultimately die by the bullets of their own comrades.

No one suspected this then. Except perhaps the two brothers themselves and the Schoolmaster. It was the Schoolmaster they came to when they escaped from Palamidi. They came disguised as herdsmen, leading a few sheep and goats. No one in the village recognized them. Time had passed, and the boys were now grown men. They strolled calmly through the town and on out toward the school. They knew the Schoolmaster usually stayed in the building even after school was over.

They left their herd outside the schoolhouse and went in. They found the Schoolmaster in the classroom. He had hung up a map on the wall, a map of the Empire of Alexander the Great. Neither one of the brothers would ever forget that map. It was the most beautiful thing they had ever seen, and they would still be able to see it in their minds when their comrades' bullets struck their hearts.

They asked the Schoolmaster to show them where Ialos was. The Schoolmaster explained that there had been no Ialos then, but that he could show them the village on another map. He spread out a new map and the brothers stared at it for a long time. They pointed to their village with their fingers.

"But it's only a name," they burst out.

"No," said the Schoolmaster. "It's not only a name. It's a thousand people. And a great many more who are now dead. And even more than that who haven't yet been born."

And suddenly the brothers knew why they were afraid. It was not the dead who frightened them. It was the unborn, all the people who would live here one day and not know a thing about the brothers or any of the rest of them either.

There was nothing you could do about the dead. But the unborn—you could do something about the unborn. The way Alexander the Great had done. You could leave a track, a vision, a scent behind you. The brothers didn't want to die until they had left something behind.

They looked out through the window. They had looked out this same window when they were little and went to school. The sun was going down. The trees in the school garden had grown. Two years had passed since they had left Ialos and the village had already changed.

Pictures rose up from their memories of the things that had marked their lives: the body of their father dangling from the chestnut tree, the naked bodies of their mother and the Lieutenant. But they also saw what they had seen as children through this window, and all of these pictures mingled with what they were seeing at that moment, and suddenly the brothers felt human. They had their memories of the past and their dreams of the future.

The sun would rise again the next morning. And the brothers would get up. But not every morning. One morning would be the last. The brothers swore a silent oath to leave their mark on the world, and the Schoolmaster sensed it. He sensed it because he had once sworn the same oath to himself. But the years had gone by and the Schoolmaster's passage through life had left its mark on himself but hardly on the world.

They all three fell into each other's arms and wept, but none of them spoke, for there was nothing to say. But there was a lot to be done, and the two brothers took their herd and walked on toward One Arm.

## PATRIOTS AND TRAITORS

There is one thing an Ialite always is. An Ialite is a patriot. Nothing can alter that fact. An Ialite is a patriot under all circumstances. If he commits treason, he does it for the good of his country. If he administers his country on behalf of a foreign power, he does so with the good of his country in mind.

Consequently there was nothing worse than calling an Ialite a traitor. He was liable to rise up in majestic wrath and strike his accuser dead. An Ialite could become very solemn on such occasions.

The fear of being looked upon as a traitor led the Ialites to make the most remarkable statements on all manner of subjects from the general worth of the Greek way of life to the current condition of the national soccer team.

Patriotism embraced not only the nation as a whole but also each of the smaller units to which an Ialite belonged. First of all, he was a patriot as a Greek, especially with reference to Bulgarians and Turks. Next, he was a patriot both as an ancient and as a modern Greek with reference to the rest of the civilized world. After that, he was patriotic about the southern Peloponnesus, about the county capital, about his own village, about the village hall, the church, the school, about his café and, finally, about his street and his own house.

This view of the world found justification in a number of proverbs that the Ialites regarded as containing all the wisdom a man could require. "If you do not love your house the roof will fall on your head," was one such proverb.

Patriotism also meant that a person refused to accept any customs or modes of thought other than those of Ialos, and that he believed the Ialites to be the cleverest people in the world. The genius of Ialos was considered to exist in highly tangible form, and the town could point to an imposing list of financial kings, big-time swindlers, gigolos, bishops, generals, and others who filled the hearts of all true Ialites with pride.

Patriotism not only meant being for something, it also meant being against something. Consequently, the Ialites had a rather low opinion of the other people from their own street, county, province, and nation. The Ialites had masses of preconceived notions about all other Greeks and could tell many anecdotes holding them up to ridicule.

People from Epiros, for example, were supposedly born to sell cakes on the streets of Athens. Epiros is one of the poorest parts of the country and has a high rate of emigration—to other countries but also to other parts of Greece. There was a period, between 1949 and 1959, when every single bootblack and cake vendor on the streets of Athens came from Epiros. Their average age was barely sixteen. Several of them would live together in a single room, and a four-room dwelling often housed up to thirty *loustri*, as they were called.

They were ridiculed by everyone, adults and children alike. They were not allowed to sit in taverns or restaurants, no one spoke to them unless it was absolutely necessary, and eventually the word *loustros*, which means "bootblack," came to be as good as a curse.

Moreover, the people of Epiros were all regarded as having big heads, called "airfields." The reason for this belief was the assumption that sooner or later all Epirites would have to carry trays of cakes on their heads, and that therefore they ought to be large and flat, i.e., like airfields.

The all-encompassing patriotism of the Ialites naturally included the suspicion that all other Greeks were potential traitors, to be treated accordingly. An Ialite seldom refrained from any sort of fiendishness if he was convinced that another Greek was a traitor, or that there were traitors in his family, or that his village or his county or his province was inhabited by traitors. The Civil War went on for a long time before it actually began.

The Germans did not know how to exploit this situation. All

the Germans knew how to do was to fill the Greeks with shame. But the English, and somewhat later the Americans, too, knew how to take advantage of this state of affairs. The Germans wanted personally to annihilate that portion of the Greek population which opposed them, and had only indifferent success. The English and Americans let the Greeks who were for them eliminate the Greeks who were against them, and that worked considerably better.

The Germans made use of quislings only with reluctance, and never in prominent positions—except for the government itself, which they permitted to be Greek. The Prime Minister was General Tsolakoglou, who had signed the capitulation.

Hitler looked with suspicion not only on those who allied themselves with the Nazis when the Germans occupied their countries, but also on the various Nazi parties established in other countries before the war began. Hitler wanted to be alone. Had he been willing to share, there is reason to believe—especially in the light of what has happened since—that, health permitting, he would still be in power today.

The Nazis insulted not only their enemies, but also their sympathizers. There were a lot of Ialites who helped the Germans, but they got their reward only much later when the war had ended and the English took over. It was at that same time that the Civil War began.

Patriots killed other patriots and traitors killed other traitors. It was thus they perceived of themselves and of others. Even in Greece there have been people who did not think in these categories, but they never lived long.

Ever since Aristides the Just, the Greek people have been misled into banishing, imprisoning, torturing, or murdering those men who were not prepared to offer their lives for local honor and glory. That was the real reason. The excuse varied, depending on what was currently selling best on the somewhat unpredictable market of human persecution. It might be atheism, Communism, witchcraft, monarchy, democracy, the higher moral values, property rights, or one of many others. There has never been a shortage of excuses, and the real reason has always been the same.

So an Ialite is a patriot, and a patriot has to have his traitors in order not to have lived his life in vain.

Ialos would soon acquire its great patriot. The man who would save the town from Communism, atheism, the international Jewish conspiracy, capitalistic exploitation, fatal disease, and sexual impotence—the Ialos Member of Parliament.

# THE LIFE AND DEATH OF A FOOL

Why does a person become the village fool? How does it come about? What sets him apart from everyone else?

Lólos, whose name differed only in accent from the adjective *lolós,* which means "crazy, foolish, madcap," was not one of those village fools who became a fool as the result of some physical defect, which was the most common path to socially acceptable foolishness.

Lolos looked like most of the other men in Ialos. He was a bit below normal height, perhaps, but he didn't seem to worry about it, and neither did anyone else.

Lolos could look a girl right in the eye and say, "He knows he's short!"

He always spoke of himself that way in the third person singular, using either the pronoun or his own name.

This manner of speaking of himself, which after all does indicate a certain self-awareness, was taken by the other townspeople to show that he was a fool. The process of becoming a village fool can very well begin with a person's observing himself and communicating his observations.

People will not tolerate a split personality, at least not for very long. Every society demands a certain minimal lack of self-awareness from its members, and if anyone fails to exhibit this minimum, he may very well slip into the company of fools. Society will thrust him out, primarily because an individual with self-awareness represents a challenge to social control. He is hard to entrap and not easy to hurt. Social control is based on forcing people to accept self-images that do not agree with the pictures they would normally have of themselves.

But with Lolos this was impossible. Lolos had a clearer picture of himself than society could ever have.

And if a society is deprived of its usual methods, if a society cannot wound a person because he is too short or too tall, too slow or too quick, too lazy or too industrious, if, in short, a society cannot injure an individual because of what he is, then it has to work out some means of injuring him for what he is not. "Madman" is the obvious solution.

Human beings fight each other with images as often as they fight each other with weapons. It is partly for this reason that poetry is such a dreaded weapon. Lolos was aware of this. And so it was not long before he began spreading the strangest rumors about himself and his family.

Lolos, who had never met his father, claimed that when he was born his father was so heartbroken the moment he saw him that he "took his eyes with him and went away." The story of his birth was one of Lolos' best numbers. He told it to anyone who would listen—how his mother had gone off to "take a big dump," how she had hidden behind some bushes and made herself comfortable and was staring absent-mindedly at the sky when suddenly Lolos popped out "like a sewer rat."

The poor woman had had to stop in the middle and call out to the other women, who were harvesting olives a short way off. When they had come and taken the child away, Lolos' mother had gone on with her "big dump."

"Lolos was born in shit," was the way Lolos used to conclude the story, alluding to his present occupation as the ass-wiper of Ialos.

His mother was still alive, but no one had ever asked her if the story was true. Lolos continued to spread anecdotes about himself until in the end he had become the village fool, but had also made himself invulnerable.

Since the German Occupation, however, Lolos' life was much altered. The fear that all the Ialites felt, even if they never expressed it, was poisoning their lives. They grew suspicious and distrustful, especially after the gendarmes and their Lieutenant began to do the Germans' bidding exactly the way they would have done for a Greek government.

For Lolos the most important part of life had disappeared. Humor had vanished in a cloud of fear, suspicion and betrayal. There were a number of songs about the Italians, but about the Germans there was only Uncle Stelios' ditty about Josef Dog, and no one dared sing that one any more.

Lolos loved people, but he couldn't live with them unless he could poke fun at them, and he couldn't do that now. He grew lonely, very lonely. He began to take long walks, and on one of these walks he found a turtle. It gave him a brilliant idea.

A short way outside the village the Germans had a large gasoline depot. Naturally it was forbidden to go near it. Lolos waited until well after dark when the generator had stopped supplying electricity to the village. (One of the German regulations was that it be turned off every night at ten o'clock.) Then, with the turtle under one arm, he sneaked up to the gasoline depot. He attached a candle to the turtle's shell and lit it. And then he ran away.

After a while the Germans caught sight of this slowly moving flame and started shooting at it. They shot more and more frantically, but the flame came steadily closer.

Meanwhile Captain Schneider had reached the depot and he ordered his men to surround the light. Corporal Josef crept into the bushes with several soldiers, and when they were close enough they threw hand grenades at the flame, which went out.

The Ialites, awakened by all the shooting, had also walked out toward the depot, expecting the Germans to capture a partisan. Everyone was very eager to see a partisan. But all the Germans captured was the turtle, and although they tried to keep it a secret, word got out, and the whole county laughed at them.

Laughter had returned to Ialos. But laughter was what the Germans could tolerate least of all. They were absolutely determined to lay their hands on the guilty party, and it was not long before they were on to Lolos' trail, in spite of the fact that quite a few Ialites had secretly been trying to suggest that they themselves had thought up the joke with the turtle.

They arrested Lolos on a Friday. He was shot by a firing squad that same afternoon. All the townspeople were ordered to be present at the execution. Lolos arrived with some bread and cheese in one hand.

"If your aim is as bad as it was at that turtle, this could take all day," he said.

But the Germans snatched away his bread and cheese and threw it on the ground. They tied his hands behind his back. And then came the order that bewildered the Ialites. They were told to parade past Lolos and spit on him.

German soldiers directed the crowd of townspeople up to the condemned man and saw to it that the order was obeyed. At first people hesitated and tried to get out of it and aimed badly, and Lolos stared straight into their eyes. But the longer it went on, the more people began to lose track of what was actually happening. The whole thing became a kind of game. People would aim at different places, some at his right ear, some at his left ear, some at his lips. Lolos had already figured out who would be the first to spit on his Crown Prince.

And his guess was right. Everyone had heard the Mayor hawking and snuffling energetically in order to collect more snot and saliva, and at last he stepped forward, took aim, and let go his shot. Soon he would be the only man left in the village with a Crown Prince.

Lolos' mother stood beside him and dried his face after every gob of spittle. There were no more tears in her eyes, and she didn't say a word. She merely stared at all the people as they spit. Her eyes were distant, she looked beyond people's faces to where she saw a great fire growing larger and larger until it threatened to engulf the whole village in smoke and flames, and her as well, and suddenly she screamed, "The fire! The fire!"

The line came to an end. The Priest came forward and asked Lolos if he wanted to make his final Communion.

"Lolos does not need it," said Lolos disdainfully. "Lolos never dies."

The Priest was somewhat taken aback, but he didn't insist. After all, Lolos was a fool. Lolos could never back out of a good joke. He died as he had lived. And there are many things worse.

That same evening the male population of the town divided itself among its three cafés and discussed the events of the day. They all talked at once and every one of them claimed to have hit Lolos with the biggest hawker.

But the Mayor was the worst, for he insisted that after his shot there had simply been no need for a firing squad, because Lolos would certainly have drowned. The Lieutenant grew expansive on the subject of what a splendid thing it was for a man to end his days before the dark mouth of a rifle, to which the Mayor objected that for his part he preferred another kind of dark mouth. This remark gave rise to great mirth and the Lieutenant could see he'd been beaten, for every conversation between Ialites had to end with the victory of one person over the other, and the most desirable victory was achieved by a good joke.

Lolos had been at the dinner table with his mother when the Germans arrested him. It was Friday. His mother was fasting. She was eating a simple dinner of wrinkled brown olives and bread that she had baked with her own hands.

She had no teeth left and had to chew her food with her gums, which over the years had become as hard and sharp as knives and flashed like knives when she opened her mouth.

Lolos looked at her with moist eyes. He could never look at her without getting a lump in his throat. It was not merely love, it was something more. Lolos missed her. The stories he told had partially deprived him of his mother. He remembered her as being young and pretty. Lolos had not grown away from his mother; it was she who had grown away from him.

She ate in a series of purposeful motions. First she captured an olive with trembling hands and softened it between her thumb and forefinger. Then she opened her mouth, thrust her head forward and upward and let her tongue glide out. On it she placed the olive and a piece of bread. It was rather like taking Communion.

She crumbled the bread and the olive by rolling them slowly around against the sharp edges of her gums. Then she thrust her head forward again, let her tongue glide out, and there lay the olive pit cleaned of its meat. She picked it up between her thumb and forefinger and threw it over her shoulder in a gesture that was very young, a gesture from her girlhood when she received the blood of Christ every day but did not want it to take root in her soul.

Now she was old, but she would still leave a lot of olive trees behind her. And she would leave Lolos behind her, too. She knew he was the village fool, and that was good. Fools led protected lives. But then they took him away. She hadn't the strength to stand beside him and watch his body fall. She disappeared up toward One Arm, screaming "The fire! The fire!" as she went.

And there was a fire within her, there was indeed. She could neither eat nor sleep nor drink. She came back later in the night and buried her son all by herself, and all by herself she sang her song of mourning.

> No branches shade me as you do, my prince,
> neither cypresses nor full-grown oaks.
>
> Show thyself, my pride, as does the sun
> when day comes to the mountains and the whole world shines.
>
> A jasmine flower went on a promenade.
> O God, give us clouds so the sun won't burn.
>
> Death often strolls in our home,
> if he comes not this year he will come the next.
>
> Sky, do not cover him, earth, weigh not on him,
> he was neither married nor engaged.
>
> As the grass always grows to the edge of the water,
> there is always pain on my lips.
>
> But now the time is past and the bitter hour is come,
> you shall take your leave of us, my slender torch.

Then she vanished again. But later, when the Civil War was raging, there were stories about an old, old woman who was always present at the big battles between the Fascist and partisan armies, and always on the partisan side. She had been wounded several times, but somehow she always escaped with her life.

The Fascist officers gave their soldiers special orders to aim for her, and they took great pains to bring her down, but Lolos' mother was invincible. She gathered the bullets from her body and made a string of beads that she played with on her wanderings.

When the Civil War was over, she came back to Ialos one night and left the string of bullets on her son's grave. No one has seen her since.

## CHILDREN'S GAMES

Ever since the days of the Metaxas dictatorship there had been a youth group in Ialos called the National Youth Organization, an all-inclusive but absolutely noncommittal name. Metaxas had created it in hopes of some day being able to draw from its cadres the real leaders of his repressive apparatus.

The organization was anything but a free association of young people who shared General Metaxas' ideals. Membership was compulsory, and every schoolchild was required to belong. Even the Schoolmaster's two older sons were members of the Ialos chapter, and whenever they came home wearing their blue uniforms and black berets, the Schoolmaster stayed in his room so he wouldn't have to see them.

The Schoolmaster made the same mistake Metaxas made. He attached far too much importance to the organization. On the other hand, neither he nor the dictator could have known exactly what it was the children spent their time doing.

It is hard to say anything definite about the organization as a whole, but the chapters in the rest of the country were probably much like the one in Ialos. The National Youth Organization (EON) was a miniature of the society the children were growing up in. With or without EON, the children would still have acquired the ideals and attitudes that made such a fertile soil for Fascism—double morality, false courage, patriotism, contempt for the weak, sexual despotism, and faith in authority.

After the Civil War, Sunday school became compulsory in Greece. Children were to be reared into good Christians, but Sunday school too was an image of the larger society. Sunday school became Fascism's fortress.

EON had a hymn, of course just as Sunday school did fifteen years later. In both cases the children took the melody and made up words of their own, which they sang in secret. The Ialos version, in two-part harmony, went like this:

We're marching, marching through the town,
all you faggots can give up your sucking.
We've got the biggest cocks around,
but we're interested only in fucking.

And then the last words of this refrain were repeated in thundering chorus "In fucking! In fucking!"

We believe in the church, we believe in God,
we believe in Greece and the King.
But most of all we believe in balls
and we're interested only in fucking.
(Refrain: We're marching etc.)

Bishops and generals are splendid men
but we'll be corporals and hunt
to find for our privates a cozy den
in the Queen's own royal cunt.
(Refrain: We're marching etc.)

After the fall of the Metaxas regime, EON was dissolved and the hymn was forgotten. It was this organization that the Ialos Member of Parliament wanted to breathe fresh life into so as to become its leader. A man had to think of the future. All he needed to do was change the name and find a new anthem. He could always attract young people with the promise of a dance or something.

He couldn't make membership in the organization compulsory, of course, but there were lots of other ways. The gendarmerie Lieutenant could help by offering the children some training in the art of warfare. That was always popular. And if he could then get a few of them to join the organization, the rest would follow by themselves.

The MP had little cause to worry. Now that the school was

closed—and it would stay closed for several more years—the young people had nothing else to do. They had finally grown tired of raiding the watermelon patch, which had always been a cherished pastime.

They would pick out the best melons, smash them against a stone, and pluck out the heart, that is to say, the ripest and reddest and coldest part, which they either ate or else mashed up in the palms of their hands and drank the juice of. The other pieces of the melon were used as projectiles for throwing at friends. The children always came home from these raids with great red blotches all over their bodies, as if they had been in the fist fight of the century.

The German Occupation brought many radical changes to the lives of the children in addition to the closing of the school. Their parents had to take part in forced labor to an ever increasing extent and no longer had time to look after them. The children had a new freedom, which, at least in the eyes of the adults, they had no use for.

The danger with unsupervised children is not that they will become wild and solitary. The danger is that they will organize themselves into packs and choose leaders by methods similar to those used in the rest of the animal kingdom.

Such packs can seldom live in harmony and friendship with each other. Their members eventually learn to mistreat the children from other packs. In the end, the whole village was divided into territories, each of them ruled by its own gang and all of them extremely risky for outside children to venture into.

The Schoolmaster, who had discussed this problem with the Lawyer, tried to do something about it, but the parents were terrified that their children would be infected by the Schoolmaster's ideas. They pointed out that since the school was closed, the Schoolmaster had no business interfering.

But when the MP announced his plan to form a young people's organization, all the Ialites were greatly relieved. The MP was a man you could trust. Even the Germans trusted him.

And the Ialites forced their children to join his group, which was called the Young Greek Solidarity Front. They dug out the old uniforms and flags from dictator Metaxas' time, and they were given permission to use the school for their meetings.

The MP made long speeches to the assembled youngsters, who then went out and marched through the village in step, which very nearly brought tears to the eyes of the Ialites who watched. At last there were Greeks on parade, not just Germans.

The Solidarity Front grew quickly, but there were a number of children who were not allowed to play, while some were forbidden by their parents from taking part—the mason's children, the Schoolmaster's, the three Jewish children, and a few others who had physical defects and therefore could hardly be included in an organization whose goal was to reshape all of Greece.

The children who were left out were severely persecuted and regularly beaten up, but in the beginning this mistreatment was fairly amateurish. The first serious incident occurred when some members of the Young Greek Solidarity Front happened to come across Reveka and Minos, the Schoolmaster's son, out in the fields.

The two of them often took walks together out to a place where the grass grew unusually high. They used to lie there side by side and watch the clouds, if there were any. If not, they would close their eyes and look at the sun through their lashes.

The Young Greeks cut Reveka's hair to form a Star of David on her head. They tied her to a tree and then raised one of her legs and tied it to a branch so she looked like a scissors. They discussed whether to fuck her or stuff a cucumber into her vagina. In the end they compromised by doing both.

Meanwhile, they had tied Minos to another tree and every now and then one of them would go over and spit on him. When they were finished with Reveka, they took Minos and tied him opposite her in exactly the same position, which made the two of them look as if they were dancing.

It was the Schoolmaster's older son, Stelios, who found them. When evening fell and they hadn't come home, he went to look for them. He knew where they usually went walking.

Later, years later, Minos described what he felt when his brother found them. "I forgot my own pain when I saw his eyes. I didn't think he loved me, what with the way he used to beat me up, but I realized then that he could have given his life for me. And I started crying, which I hadn't done while the whole thing was going on."

Stelios was a headstrong young man. Calmly and quietly, he took the children home and asked them not to tell anyone what had happened. The children obeyed and thought up an excuse for being late. They went to bed early, and only then did Reveka start to cry.

Stelios went out again that same night, and took his knife. The next morning three of the Young Greeks were found bleeding badly behind some bushes. Stelios was nowhere to be found, and no one saw him again for several years.

He headed off in the same direction David Kalin had taken a few months earlier. He was planning to make his way to the mainland and join the guerrilla army of Ares Velouchiotis. All he took with him was the bloody knife and the bloody cucumber that he himself had pulled from Reveka's hairless vagina.

Armed groups had already been formed in northern Greece. One of the most legendary leaders, Communist Ares Velouchiotis, retreated up into the mountains almost immediately after the capitulation and soon he had built a considerable partisan force.

Velouchiotis was later murdered on the orders of Nikos Zachariadis, the General Secretary of the Communist Party. The problem was that Velouchiotis opposed the Varkiza agreement whereby ELAS, the Greek resistance army, turned over its weapons to Georgios Papandreou's government and thus to the English.

The Varkiza agreement was unique in that conservatives and Communists together agreed, in practice, to sell Greece to the English. Zachariadis was following orders from the Kremlin and Papandreou from London, but Velouchiotis thought for himself. He thought about the Greek people, and he died young. It has always been hard to keep track of the patriots and traitors in Greece.

The death of Velouchiotis was a great loss to the Party, but an even greater loss to the partisan army, which was deprived of one of its most capable leaders. Moreover, the last thirty years of history have shown that Velouchiotis was absolutely right. The resistance should not have laid down its arms. It should have kept them and negotiated with weapons in hand. In that case Greece might be an independent nation today, rather than a base for the

American fleet, which is what Greece will remain until more men like Ares, as the people called him, appear and survive, or anyway escape being murdered by their own people.

But at this time, Velouchiotis was still alive. His guerrilla name —his real name was Thanasis Klaras—was on people's lips all over Greece. Stories about him spread. They told about his horse and about his long, black beard. They told about his men, who never left his side.

A lot of young men left their homes and villages at night and headed into the mountains, for Ares had succeeded in doing what had to be done in order to accomplish anything in Greece. He had given the Greeks back their pride.

Stelios planned to join Ares but he never had to go that far. Up in the Taigetos Mountains near Sparta he found a group consisting of David Kalin, a secondary-school teacher from another village, an ex-corporal, a gendarme who had deserted, and, to his amazement, the Circuit Magistrate.

The Magistrate was tired of being a judge. He no longer had the strength. In the course of his whole career there had been only a few brief periods when he could judge in accordance with his own principles. But this was the last straw. He would not work for the Germans, too.

He realized that his sisters would never marry. He realized that he would soon die, on a dishonorable pension paid him by the Greek people for services that were largely directed against them. And, finally, he realized that he wanted to be part of this movement, which would create new songs. He would no longer collect the old ones. He would write the new songs himself.

Down in the valley it was still a mild fall. But up in the Taigetos Mountains it was winter.

## HUNGER

The winter of 1941 was to be the coldest in years. But it was not only cold. For the embattled German armies it also meant a change in the fortunes of war. The Germans had reached Moscow, but there they bogged down. More and more forces had to be sent to the Russian front. The supervision of the occupied countries could no longer be carried out with the same efficiency. War weariness began to spread among the German soldiers.

For Greece it was a winter of hunger. By late summer, foodstuffs had already vanished from the market. The shops closed. People tried to hoard and hide food, but it couldn't be done. The German and Italian armies needed all the provisions they could lay their hands on. By early winter, starvation was a fact.

Athens and Pireus suffered most. People collapsed on the streets and no one had the strength to help them up. They lay on the sidewalks and died. There was a terrible stench in both cities. Trucks drove around fighting to keep the streets clean.

German and Italian soldiers marched among decaying corpses. They sang their songs, and their weapons gleamed, but it wasn't the way it had been. They were obviously in the grip of exhaustion and despair.

This naturally led to an intensification of the hunt for Communists, Jews, and other dangerous types. Raids were carried out day and night. Whole blocks were obliterated. Mass arrests alternated with mass executions, and in the meantime people were starving to death. In the winter of '41, about half a million people in Athens and Pireus died of starvation.

Those who were young enough and strong enough headed for

the mountains. It was one way of escaping starvation. Children and old people moved out to their relatives in the country, if they had any. Everyone else had to depend on the black market.

Fortunes were exchanged for a few loaves of bread and a couple of liters of olive oil. When the war was over, the profiteers who had acquired these fortunes would make up the backbone of the growing middle class. In spite of being persecuted, the Greek Communist Party managed to form committees against starvation. These committees helped those who could not help themselves, and, as far as possible, they punished the black-market sharks.

A new profession came into being that winter—the so-called *saltadóri*, people who specialized in stealing from supply depots and from passing wagons and trains and trucks, people who caught cats and sold them as rabbits, people who slaughtered stolen horses and donkeys and sold them on the black market.

It was a profession that required courage, skill, and a heart like a cash register. Many of the older businessmen that tourists today see dozing outside their shops were once saltadóri. But time passes quickly. People forget. The saltadóri become merchants, and the Occupiers become tourists, and those who were occupied become guest laborers in the occupying country.

But 1941 was no year for tourists. Although some people did move around. Several families came to Ialos from Athens and Pireus. Driven out of the city by hunger, they thought of their relatives in the country. These relatives were often very distant, but they went to them anyway.

And the Ialites took in these refugees—maybe not with open arms exactly, but they did take them in. Because hunger had reached even Ialos, and people sensed what it was like to lie to children who wanted food, and to lie to yourself and tell yourself that tomorrow you were certain to find something.

Of course there never was as much starvation in the countryside as in the cities. The farmers had learned to make use of every nutritious plant. They could make bread out of weeds and squeeze oil from a stone.

The Schoolmaster organized a committee with the Lawyer and one of the masons. They collected all the food they could lay their hands on and parceled it out to those who needed it most. The

Ialites started calling the Schoolmaster "Mr. Vitamin," because he was always telling them about the vitamins in all of the plants they had previously considered worthless.

Dandelions could be dried and made into a nourishing soup. Coffee could be made from acorns. Almonds contained a very rich oil, and there were a lot of almond trees in Ialos.

The sense of community increased among the Ialites. They seemed to require hard and unhappy times in order to display any kind of solidarity.

People had always been afraid of the man who owned the slaughterhouse, but now he became a ministering angel. He went out every day and hunted hares and rabbits without a gun, because guns were prohibited. All he had was a knife. He would hide behind a bush and wait for a hare to happen by and then throw the knife at it. He threw with great strength and accuracy and seldom missed.

Old man Mousouris shared his wealth. He considered it a personal disgrace for his village to be starving, so he opened his cellars to everyone, although there was very little left. The Germans had already taken most of it.

In all of this the Lawyer found confirmation of his theory that friendship constituted the spiritual focus of the Greek character, which he took the opportunity of pointing out to the Schoolmaster.

"You see, we're not like the rats. We don't eat each other when we're hungry."

The Schoolmaster's family was in the worst position of all. He had no land. He had a salary that was no longer being paid, since after all the school was closed. And moreover he had a son who had disappeared. The Germans were keeping an eye on him, as were the Mayor and the gendarmes.

The Schoolmaster expected to be arrested at any moment. He knew the Germans would come knocking on his door some night, but he couldn't leave his family. The Germans did come, and the Schoolmaster managed to escape out the back way. But when he was a short distance from the village, he found he could not go on. He turned back.

The Germans were sitting in the big room, waiting. Minos and Reveka were huddled next to his wife. His oldest son had run away the night before. The Schoolmaster looked at his wife and the children.

"Why?" his wife said, meaning why had he come back.

"I don't know," the Schoolmaster said, and that was true.

But his wife had known he would come back. She had a bundle of clothing already packed for him. The Germans stood up. The Schoolmaster's wife picked up a string of dried figs that she had been saving for a long time and stuffed it in among his clothes.

"Will you be all right?" he asked.

"We're not alone," she whispered.

They would not see each other again for five years.

## THE CHRISTMAS PARTY

Christmas drew near, and the Greeks, who, like other people, are somewhat sentimental about Christmas, began to groan and complain.

"Christmas in slavery and hunger! What kind of Christmas is this?"

But their downheartedness did not last long. The Greeks discovered that even the Germans grew sentimental around Christmas, despite the fact that things were not going well for them in Russia. The name of Russia was often mentioned with respect in those days, just as it had been a hundred years earlier. After all, it said in the Apocalypse that the red nation would conquer the world.

"No, Hitler's boys are going to get themselves thrashed by the muzhiks. Nobody can beat the muzhiks. Even Napoleon discovered that."

The Ialites went around being very pleased at the German setbacks. Gradually they began to perceive decisive differences between the Germans and the Russians. Stalin had a mustache that any real man might envy. Hitler had a bird turd on his upper lip. Where did he get the nerve to call that thing a mustache? It was a wonder he wasn't struck by lightning.

The Ialites chose a delegation—with the Mayor as its chairman—to request extra rations from the Germans so that they could celebrate Christmas "in keeping with the national traditions of the Greek people."

Captain Schneider, who was no idiot, knew enough to treat them with respect—at least this once. The Ialites needn't worry.

They would have their Christmas food. He also promised an amnesty, though he would have to give some more thought to its scope.

The German Captain was a rather peculiar man. He must have been tired of the war long before it began. He was about fifty years old and had a very distinct face in the sense that every single feature was immediately conspicuous.

Eyes, lips, nose, ears, cheeks—you noticed everything at once. It usually takes months before you notice, say, a person's ears. Schneider was unpredictable, but not as strict as other German officers were rumored to be. He was said to have had a good laugh when he heard the song about Josef Dog.

He had just been planning a big Christmas party for his men and had secretly been wondering how he could get the Ialites to come. A man had to have a few women around at Christmas or he felt like one more sausage among sausages. So he was very happy about the Ialites' request. Now they would not only come to the party, they would even be grateful.

"The people should love their masters," he used to say to his lieutenant.

The days passed and Christmas came closer. German soldiers were seen arriving with great bags and sacks and cases of food. The Ialites' mouths watered. The first Christmas in slavery and hunger was a Christmas everyone looked forward to impatiently.

The party was to be held in the schoolhouse, where there was plenty of space. Moreover, it had a small room where the officers and the town authorities could be by themselves.

The women of Ialos spent several days helping with the preparations, and for the first time in their lives they saw a Christmas tree, which the Germans had decorated in their traditional manner. People didn't have Christmas trees in Greece, not then.

Christmas Eve arrived and the Priest read the Gospel at breakneck speed. He stumbled over the words as if they'd been bushes on broken ground. The congregation rushed from the church and practically ran to the schoolhouse.

First the German Captain made a speech in which he emphasized the importance of German-Greek friendship. The translation was handled by a special interpreter, so Uncle Stelios missed the chance of having a little fun with the Ialites.

Then the Mayor made a short speech in which he emphasized the importance of Greek-German friendship, and then it was every man for himself. The Ialites raced headlong for the huge table, and the Priest was heard to curse at the top of his lungs that some son-of-a-bitch had tripped him.

There was plenty of wine, but the Ialites were not interested in drinking. It was the food they had their eyes on. When they were finished eating and had reached that pleasant stage where a man can concentrate on his digestion, small sounds began to be heard from all over the room—belches that could hardly be suppressed and discreet farts that nevertheless drew some comment either from the guilty party—"Uh-oh, I just cut one." Or from his neighbor at table—"Okay, who the hell lost his cork?" and so forth.

The Ialites often felt a great tenderness for their own basic functions, though not always. It was only when they were full and happy. "My home is my castle," says the Englishman, but the Ialite says, "My body is my castle."

The Greco-German festive table offered a combination of dishes that was like nothing ever seen before. Rich German cuisine with its butter, ham, potatoes, and heavy pastries, together with the mutton, lemons, olives, and Turkish sweets of the Greek kitchen.

The Ialites helped themselves to everything indiscriminately, and some people's plates looked like Towers of Babel as they left the table carrying their booty high above their heads. Naturally accidents occurred. People poured wine or soup on their neighbors.

When the food had disappeared, they all began to drink. Everyone was already fairly groggy from eating, so it didn't take them long. The result was general brotherhood, communal song, and Josef Dog was seen dancing with Uncle Stelios.

The bigwigs sat by themselves and preserved their dignity. The Mayor could not restrain himself, however, and time and again he came out into the main room for a swing with one of the girls.

The German soldiers hugged the Greek girls tight, and the girls, who liked nice-smelling blond young men, hugged them back—although with a certain reserve.

The night wore on. It was hours since the birth of Jesus and hours since the Priest had fallen asleep, and still the dancing continued. But the Schoolmaster's house was silent and lonely. The Schoolmaster's wife neither dared nor wanted to go to the party. The promised amnesty had come into effect, but it did not include her husband. She and Reveka and Minos sat together in the kitchen. They could hear the roars of festivity coming from the schoolhouse from where they had once heard the shouts of children, and she had to wipe an occasional tear from her eye. But Reveka had an unusual gift for detecting tears, and comforted her.

"He'll come back, you'll see. My Mama and Papa will come home, too, and then Minos and I will get married."

There has never yet been a Greek mother who failed to brighten up at the mention of marriage. Reveka had once again said the right thing.

Suddenly there was a knock at the door. Their hearts stopped beating. She would have to answer it. There came another knock, not hard, but firm. She went to the door.

"Who is it?"

"It is I, Kiriakos."

She opened the door, and there stood the Gendarmerie Commander, Kiriakos Halakis. He was the last person who should have had any contact with the Schoolmaster's family. But the Lieutenant and the Schoolmaster had secretly been friends. The Schoolmaster played the violin quite well, and the Lieutenant was good on the Cretan lyre. They had often played together. The music of Crete and the music of Pontos were similar, and the combination of the two instruments and the two traditions had given them a lot of pleasure. Halakis had come as a friend. He had set aside a little food and wine and merely wanted to wish them Merry Christmas.

The poor woman burst into tears. The Lieutenant was also moved and began to chew on his mustache the way he always did. And he had a real mustache, not a bird turd like Hitler's.

## CONSEQUENCES

The party went off without any serious conflicts between the Germans and the Ialites. And nevertheless, there were certain consequences. One consequence was that the Captain and the Lieutenant were sent to the Eastern Front. Josef Dog took over.

Another was that several romances developed between German soldiers and the daughters of villagers, and this threw Ialos into a state of moral indignation. There was a limit, after all. No one had any business going to bed with a German when there were still plenty of Greeks available. If the Germans had brought along a few of their own women so the Ialites could have had a taste, at least, but no. The German cunts were all at home in Germany, baking rolls and knitting socks.

Under the weight of moral pressure, most of these relationships soon came to an end, but there was one of the girls who could not tear herself away from her German. The reason was quite simple. She was expecting his child. And so the time for the first tragedy had arrived.

Several members of the Young Greek Solidarity Front, which among its other duties also attended to the preservation of morality, kidnaped the girl one night and cut off all her hair with sheep shears.

Of course the girl did not dare to go home with that kind of sheepish skull. She chose instead to throw herself into a well and attempt to reach God by that route.

The Ialites showed no mercy toward the girl or toward her family. In the first place, she was expecting a baby with a German. In the second place, if a person was going to commit suicide, there was no need to poison a well in the process. What the hell did they have the chestnut tree for?

Her relatives, however much they may have grieved, exhibited no public emotion that was not in keeping with the over-all moral framework of the town. They were at least as indignant as everyone else at the girl's behavior. It was just as well that she was gone, and that she had seen to it herself.

But the man who was the cause of her death and the family's dishonor lived on, despite the fact that the girl had three brothers and a considerable number of cousins. He lived, and was already chasing another girl.

He was about twenty years old, unusually well built, and had long scandalized the town. For he used to bathe naked in the town fountain every day at siesta time, summer and winter alike. The girls of Ialos would lower the blinds and stand behind them to enjoy the sight of his splendid organ, which he always lathered with especial care. He would draw its foreskin back and forth until finally it stood there naked and clean beneath the enslaved Greek sky.

This behavior did arouse a certain moral indignation among the Ialites, and yet it was such an odd element in the life of the village that it somehow seemed unreal. But the young man became extremely real when his mistress took her own life. He should have known better, but he did not.

One morning Ialos was poorer by four people. The girl's three brothers had disappeared and the German soldier lay dead in a little cave from which the townspeople had often smoked out foxes. The brothers had stuffed a lemon in his mouth, as if he had been a pig. And his penis was missing—this too as if he had been a pig.

Six months after the arrival of the Germans, Ialos could boast the following statistics: six men in the mountains, one in prison, one at Dachau, fifteen men doing forced labor at the airfield, five men doing forced labor outside Sparta. The confectioner's two sons were also in the mountains, but no one in Ialos knew that. One man had been shot by a firing squad, and four men had been beaten. All without the inhabitants of Ialos having committed any acts of opposition in the true sense of the word.

When the Germans, with the help of their German shepherd,

found the murdered soldier, Josef Dog flew into a rage. He ordered all the men over sixteen to assemble in the village square. The bell ringer had to ring his bells frenetically until every one of them stood facing Josef Dog. They lined up obediently, three by three, with no idea of what was in store for them.

Josef Dog stood in the middle of the square. With no trace of mercy in his eyes he pointed to every third man, and they were immediately snatched out of line by German soldiers. He didn't bother to find out who had killed his soldier. For every German life, ten Greeks would pay with theirs—that was the rule. Except of course for those cases when a German life might cost a couple of hundred Greek lives. Now that Josef was sole master of Ialos, he would show the townspeople what the Thousand Year Reich was to be built upon—corpses and more corpses, and on top of them an SS soldier with a clean-shaven face.

The women, who had slowly been gathering in the square as well, realized that murder was afoot. The men weren't so quick to understand. The women rushed to their men and tried to pull them out of line, but the German soldiers knocked them aside.

The ten men chosen were: Mousouris' son, the third mason, three peasants from the Lower Town, the postman, David Kalin's son, the Lawyer, a carpenter, and a traveling salesman who happened to be in Ialos that day.

The Germans loaded them onto a truck and drove off toward the chestnut tree. Women, children, and the rest of the men ran after them. Clouds of dust rose in their path. No one spoke. No one shrieked or wept. By the time they reached the tree, the ten men were already dead. The chestnut tree shaded their bodies. The truck had already driven away.

Then a great cry arose from all those breasts. The sky darkened, the leaves of the chestnut trembled, and the people's voices became like the wind, full of grief and rage.

People in Ialos still talk about that execution, especially when the postman is mentioned, because he had six unmarried sisters to take care of. These sisters grieved visibly and audibly for weeks. The sound of sobbing could be heard from their house both night and day, in spite of the fact that the windows were closed and shuttered.

On a single day, the mirrors in ten houses were covered with black cloth. On a single day, a great many different women saw their brothers, husbands, and sons lie in the dust with silent, bleeding mouths.

Reveka was one of the very few who did not rush to the chestnut tree. She knew what the dead looked like. She did not want to see her brother dead. She would not believe it anyway. She sat by herself in the children's silent bedroom. She had drawn the shades, and she sat in the semi-darkness and thought about the cherry tree her father had planted when Markus was born.

The tree bore fruit now. Its roots had made their way deep into the soil and one day—of this she was certain—one day the roots would reach all the way to Markus' bed in the earth and then one of two things would happen: either the cherry tree, too, would die, or else Markus would come back to life, smiling with all thirty-three of his teeth.

Markus had one tooth too many, and his two sisters used to tease him about it. Reveka wept silently.

From outside in the sun she could hear the desperate voices of the other women. She could hear the churning sound of nails tearing their cheeks and scalps. She could hear the sound of tears bursting through the vaults of their eyes with a quiet detonation.

But when they gathered the bodies in the church—in the Christian church—in order to wash them and dress them and read over them, Reveka went. She was at a loss about what to do. Their God was not hers and Markus'. But Markus no longer needed any God, and it might make him feel better to be washed along with the others, and to rest with the others.

Why do people need a God when they have each other, Reveka wondered, and she joined in the work with the other women.

Outside the church, the German soldiers played soccer. As goals they used four peasants, who had to stand without moving for as long as the game lasted. But the soccer-hungry goal posts couldn't always keep themselves out of the game and were often seen to use their heads and feet and even to run out to intercept the ball. The Germans would laugh, not really understanding why a peasant couldn't even be a goal post without committing breaches of discipline.

The Greek peasants would never gain entry to the Thousand Year Reich. Not alive in any case.

Josef Dog had lost the battle, but he didn't know that. Of those he spared, the majority vanished up into the mountains as quickly as they could. The ones who stayed were the ones who had no other choice. Some of them became Josef's dogs. Among them was the Mayor, whom Josef first dismissed and then reinstated.

The Mayor got money from Josef and organized a little troop of armed men. This was the beginning of the famous Security Battalions, Greek groups armed and organized by the Germans in many different parts of the country. But it was too late. The war was not going at all the way Hitler had expected. Alliances with the Germans were becoming more and more inopportune. Moscow did not fall. German troops were retreating from the Soviet Union. It seemed likely that the Red Army would soon come storming down into the Balkans and Central Europe. The resistance movements in the occupied countries had grown. The Allied air forces were already bombing right in the middle of Germany and the occupied territories.

But Josef Dog thought his position was quite secure. He had the valley at his feet and all of his machine guns, submachine guns, and grenade launchers directed down into it. He didn't reckon with One Arm. It did not occur to him that it could be climbed. But he was wrong.

One morning when the Ialites woke up they saw the Greek flag flying from the highest limb of the fig tree on top of One Arm. It waved in the breeze, and on it they could clearly read the letters EAM-ELAS. These were the initials of the Greek liberation army. The resistance had begun in earnest.

## PARTISANS

In Ialos, very little was known about the partisans and the way they lived. There were people, of course—especially shepherds—who claimed to have met partisans and who could supply information about them. But they made most of it up.

In the beginning, the partisans had as little contact as possible with the civilian populace. Partly to protect themselves from informers and partly to create the impression that the partisan army was large. An invisible army is always believed to be larger than it really is.

Social reform, at least for the majority of the populace, is never based on an objective analysis of reality. Reforms must somehow grow out of myths, that is to say, out of the ideas and beliefs that have an emotional foothold among the people.

Tragically, the individuals who have this emotional purchase on the people—kings, generals, bishops—are, as a rule, opposed to the people and their interests. And while it is true that the revolution must begin among the people, it is also true that the people regard their peers with great suspicion.

It was essential for the partisans to create new myths. One step in this direction was for them to change their identities, and this was most simply done by changing their names. An ordinary Thanasis Klaras became Ares Velouchiotis. Ares was the ancient Greek god of war, and Velouchi was a high and very beautiful mountain. Of course they changed their names partly as a security measure. But the very choice—conscious or unconscious—of names that had associations to tradition, myth, folk song, and landscape indicated precisely this desire to avoid the commonplace, for fear that the people would not find the partisans inspiring.

Naturally, these assumed names also told something about their owners. A great deal of poetry was written in those days by changing names. The man fighting up in the hills was no longer Giorgákis, the shepherd. At one time or another, almost everyone had boxed Giorgákis' ears. No, now his name was Nikiforos—he who brings victory—and he had a beard that hung down to his knees.

A revolution that isn't based on mythology and that doesn't build its own mythology can never succeed. Although no amount of mythology can guarantee success, since after all mythology can't defeat a superior army. Moreover, the people with the weapons usually also have the myths—the myths that can be forced on people by weapons.

The people have been misled for quite some time now. They have learned to shout "Democracy!" when they should be shouting "Food and clothing!" They have learned to shout "Freedom and justice!" when they ought to be shouting "Food and clothing!" again. They have learned to shout "Jobs for everyone!" as if labor were a privilege. This is the ideological double standard on which our world is built.

The Greek resistance movement was free of this double standard in the beginning. The people wanted their harvests, their food, their homes, and more and more of them joined the partisans. But then along came the intellectuals. They brought Marx's slippers, and the people's dirty, tired feet were supposed to fit them. The Greek resistance movement was to become a Marxist resistance movement. It should have stayed Greek, because that was the only way to keep it unified. And so far the people were taking up arms not to defend their *right* to survival but only in order to survive. And time passed.

Josef Dog ran amuck in Ialos. Every time the partisans showed themselves in the mountains he sent more men into forced labor or to concentration camps. There were many families in mourning in the village, but it was the grief of Mousouris that stood out, just as formerly it had been his happiness.

The wealthy old farmer was not the same man. Since his son's death he had aged with terrible speed. He couldn't let himself weep all day the way his wife did. Nor could he let himself lose his mind, which he was on the verge of doing every time he walked into his son's room and saw his clothes still hanging on their hangers, and his hunting rifle, and his soft black leather boots.

He had to swallow his heart every time he heard his son's horse whinny for its master. He often went into the stall with the beautiful animal and stroked it and stood there at a loss for what to do. He wanted to have the horse shot, for a horse like that was no real horse without its rider. But the old man couldn't bring himself to do it. He could share his grief more easily with the horse than with people.

He couldn't reach his wife—whom he still loved. Her grief was altogether too vast and deep. But the townspeople too missed the lithe figure of young Mousouris. They were used to seeing him ride by like another St. George. They were used to being awakened by the proud sound of his horse's hoofs when he was out hunting early in the morning.

The town had grown one image poorer, and that is a great deal. People wondered what old Mousouris would do. Everyone knew how stubborn he was, and they were all convinced that he would hold onto his grief the same way he held onto his land. People were afraid he might set fire to the whole village, and he almost did, too, for Mousouris was in despair.

Even though he knew that no vengeance could give him back his son. Thousands of German lives would not be enough. His world had fallen apart, and nothing could put it back together.

He would sit on his balcony with his pipe and look out over his property, and the tears would stream down his cheeks, and his grandchildren would be as silent as only children can be. They would bring a hot coal and light their grandfather's pipe and then wait for the old man to discover them again.

"God damn it to hell!"

This exclamation, directed at nothing in particular, burst from Mousouris in his sleep and woke him. He struggled up out of bed and repeated it, this time cursing the fact that he had woken himself up.

If at least he could remember what the dream had been about.

There were dreams that frightened him even though there was nothing in them that was frightening. Sometimes they were even rather idyllic. But it was the way the dreams took shape—they came as totalities, like blocks of stone.

He would see a whole story at once as if it were painted on a wall, like the murals in church. And he would move passively from one scene to the next without doing anything, and no one else did anything either. It was like wandering through a museum that had been built in weightless space.

Since the death of his son there had been substantial changes in the old man's sleeping habits. He would fall asleep in one dream and wake up in another. As a result he thought he was awake all the time. He longed for sleep, and he was old enough not to fear death. Or maybe death had lost its hold on him.

For many years Mousouris had thought of death as a kind of sleep. He could hardly see the difference any more.

"Well, the old man's going to have a cup of coffee," he decided, in a voice that was neither low enough to give the impression he was talking to himself nor loud enough for anyone else to hear. His voice had acquired a middle level, an evasive coloration that no one reacted to, not even he. So meager could a man become with the years.

Mousouris recalled his dead mother. Toward the end of her life she had been nothing but skin and bone. She had grown so unbelievably thin, almost transparent, that she made mistakes about her own body. She walked and believed she was standing still. She had to ask other people if she had moved or not.

She suspected that it was God who had willed this change, for if she was to fall she would have to be light in body, regardless of whether she fell up or down.

For her, death was somehow the same as falling, and she used to joke about it with a song she called The Falling Song:

> Death came to me one night
> and gave me a shove on the chest.
> I fell down like a crust of bread.
> Death took the crumbs,
> and I took the wine.
> Cheers!

And the old woman finally did meet her maker in a fall. She was putting up new curtains when she fell from the ladder and broke several ribs and her neck.

Mousouris went out to the kitchen. He forgot why he was there and stood looking out the window. Dawn was coming. The night mist was floating across the fields like linen sheets—the earth about to get out of bed. From the stable he could hear the horse, his son's horse. Mousouris put on a coat and went out to visit the horse. When he went to stroke it he discovered a knife in his right hand. He remembered that he'd been going to cut himself a piece of bread in the kitchen, but suddenly the kitchen was far away, very far away, and he could never go back to the kitchen. He led the horse outside and saddled it and managed to get on. He rode down toward the village. He passed several peasants who crossed themselves in the belief that they had seen a ghost. Mousouris rode straight down to the German barracks. He reigned in the horse, took a deep breath, and shouted, "Josef, if you are a man, come out!"

The Ialites watched in horror from behind their windows. Josef came out. Of course he didn't understand what Mousouris had shouted. The horse leaped toward him like a gust of wind. The German guard fired a burst from his submachine gun, and both Mousouris and the horse fell over backward. Josef Dog turned deathly pale. The Ialites prayed silently. And a new day dawned.

## TO THE SPARTA PRISON

Several months had passed since the Germans arrested the Schoolmaster and no one had heard a word from him, although there were several different rumors about his fate.

According to some reports, he had already been executed. According to others, he had been sent to a concentration camp in Germany. According to still others, he had escaped and was up in the mountains with David and the partisans.

His wife lived in uncertainty. She often cried at night when the children had gone to bed, but during the day she was as happy as a wagtail. "The children shouldn't have to comfort me," she thought. "They need to be comforted themselves."

For Reveka and Minos, the Schoolmaster's absence meant a new emptiness. The Schoolmaster had shown them all kinds of plants and trees and animals. He had taken them out on the terrace on summer nights and told them the names of the different stars. The Schoolmaster had had a name for everything, and the children felt secure in a world of names. But now the world was nameless. There was no one to ask. And no one could answer.

Reveka and Minos had to put together their own world, but it didn't satisfy them. A child that knows it can find out for certain is not satisfied with made-up names.

Every evening when they went to bed and prayed to their separate Gods, they prayed for two things—bread for the next day, and the return of the Schoolmaster. Reveka had already learned to pray silently, which is the first step toward not praying at all, but Minos wanted to have no secrets with his God. He spoke loudly and clearly, and when he had finished his prayer he would call out to his mother, "Now I've prayed again. We'll see what happens!"

But nothing happened. Days went by, and weeks, and months, and bread became more and more scarce, and the Schoolmaster did not return. It was then Minos showed his first atheistic tendency. He defied his God.

"Either my father comes home or else you're not my God!"

His grandmother happened to hear this piece of attempted blackmail and was absolutely beside herself. It must have been one of the few times she ever went red in the face, for otherwise she was always very pale. In order to save her grandchild from his incipient atheism she decided to go out and look for the Schoolmaster "in every corner of the world," as she put it.

Thus her pilgrimage began. She simply took to the road. She asked everyone she met. She stopped in every village, at every cottage, at every farm. She had a picture of the Schoolmaster and also one of his wife, her daughter.

She would take out the Schoolmaster's picture, which she kept hidden under all her skirts, and show it to the peasants, and each time she did she could see that the picture had faded slightly. Finally there were only traces left of the Schoolmaster's lean face. She saw this as a good omen. The fading of the picture could mean that the Schoolmaster himself was wasting away somewhere—in some prison perhaps—but it also meant he wasn't dead.

On the road she met many other women who were out on the same errand—looking for a husband, a son, a brother, or some other close relative. Some of them had children at their breasts, others had them in their bellies, and some were much too old to have or to hope for a child.

These women recognized each other at a glance. Nothing makes people easier to identify than a great sorrow. Their clothing, their walk, their eyes—all these things betrayed them to the Germans but also revealed them to one another. They shared their bread and their olives. They shared a blanket for the night, and they shared the dust on the gravel roads.

They walked on and on, but in an occupied country no one ever gets far. Barbed wire, closed roads, military patrols, guard posts, and signs forbidding their presence were everywhere. They walked and walked as if in a labyrinth. They found themselves back at their starting points or wound up in cul-de-sacs.

These flocks of women with their common sorrow crossed the whole of Greece and crossed it again, but most of them never found what they were looking for. There was no one who knew anything, although everyone could tell something he had heard from someone who had heard it from someone else, and so on.

Despair creates its own myths, and grief forces people to believe in them. The women wandered about, grasped every new rumor and pursued it until they were back where they had started. Along the way, new women joined the group. In the end there were almost fifty of them. Walking along the dusty roads they looked like a giant black snake gliding slowly from village to village.

It was not long before the superstitious peasants began to see them as the cause of various unwelcome occurrences. In the beginning they were understanding and tried to help the women, but as time passed and the number of women grew and the trek moved on through the German-built labyrinth, aversion toward them steadily increased.

First people refused to give them anything to eat and drink. Then they stopped letting them sleep in barns and sheepfolds. In the end they wouldn't even let them pass through their villages. They had no compassion left for the "red widows," as they were called.

A lot of "red widows" gave up and headed back for their own villages. Some of them never made it, but lay down under a tree somewhere and died. But the Schoolmaster's mother-in-law never gave up. The dreadful prospect of seeing her grandchild become an atheist filled her with a terrible strength that no one had ever suspected her thin, sickly body could possess.

She ate roots that she dug as she went along. She slept wherever she could, but never more than a couple of hours at a time. Her eyes grew even larger than they had been, and they had been large to begin with. Her thin body grew even thinner, and she was racked by coughing. But she went on. She found her son-in-law in the Sparta prison.

"When I saw the walls, everything went black before my eyes," she said later. "So I realized he must be inside. And I realized I would have to wait outside those walls until they opened for me."

They let her in. She waited outside the prison gates day and night, dressed in black, her gaze dry and burning, and finally the

Germans couldn't stand it any more. None of the guards had ever seen her sleep or eat or drink.

She sat on a stone across from the gate with her head in her hands and rocked back and forth as if she were holding a baby. She rocked like a clock afraid of stopping at the wrong hour.

Many years later the Schoolmaster told how the old woman—who had not shed a tear on her whole journey—wept uncontrollably when she finally saw him. She was embarrassed that she had nothing to bring him. Nothing but the picture of her daughter, his wife. Then she fainted.

She was examined by a doctor—a Greek who was also a prisoner—and he said that she should have been dead weeks ago. But she wasn't ready to die. She had to get all the way back home. And so she walked back to Ialos. She had gathered dust all over the province, but it was only when she had told her daughter and Minos that their husband and father was alive and in good health, and that he had sent them many kisses, it was only then that she lay down and closed her eyes.

But she wasn't allowed to die. Her husband—Stelios the jokester—went into the biggest act of his career and began singing songs in an unidentifiable language he insisted was Chinese. He walked about the house at all hours of the day and night, singing in a nasal voice that would have raised the dead like flies in a suddenly warmed room.

The old woman simply could not die under such circumstances. She dragged herself out of bed, ate a little food and drank a little wine, which made her terribly drunk, of course, and by and by both husband and wife could be heard singing a song Stelios had made up to ridicule death.

Death, oh Death, come quick,
so you can lick my prick.
Oh Death, don't be so fussy,
come out and lick my pussy.
Oh tra la la la lee
the world was made for me.

The old couple were to live for many more years, and in the meantime Minos would become not only an atheist but a Communist and a libertine as well.

## THE TRIANGLE OF SILENCE

Among the families that came to Ialos from Athens during the famine, there was one that consisted of only a mother and daughter. The father had been shot by a firing squad at Haidari, a camp outside Athens. Thirty years later, in the early hours of the twenty-first of April, Greek armor would leave Haidari to carry out another occupation of the country.

Haidari, Skopeftiri, Bouboulinas Street—all these places that have survived a resistance war and a civil war. Places where Greeks have been tortured, imprisoned, and executed, by other Greeks as well as by Germans.

It makes a person wonder what a people has to do to gain its freedom.

"Fight," say the poet and the revolutionary. But they both feel they've done their duty as soon as the former has written a poem and the latter has passed it out.

Fight, yes. The Greeks have fought. But a person can fight for the wrong freedom, too. He can fight to bring back the monarchy. He can fight to defend a dictatorship. He can fight to achieve his own humiliation.

Mother and daughter had had enough fighting. The mother had been watching her husband go off to different prisons ever since 1918. His imprisonment had been interrupted by brief periods of freedom, during which he always threw himself back into the struggle, only to find himself in prison once again.

She had seen her brothers sent to prisons and deportation camps. And finally she had had to bury them, one after the other. In a single year she threw handfuls of earth into four different graves.

No, she had had enough fighting. Now she was going to sit in her kitchen and mourn her dead and rest her eyes on her daughter, who in the meantime had grown to be a wonderfully beautiful girl.

The daughter's name was Karina. Her father had loved boats and was an atheist. He hadn't wanted to give his daughter a biblical name, so he called her Karina, which means "keel." The name was something of a sensation to the Ialites, for whom the word had a different connotation. Specifically, it was the name of a position used in sexual intercourse to avoid conception.

Karina was beautiful in a way that fell outside the villagers' criteria for beauty. She was tall. She had long legs that filled out as they reached her hips, which were unusually high. Her waist was small, and the line of her back curved first inward—just deeply enough to delay a caress—and then outward again toward her shoulders and long neck. Her hair fell in great curls all the way to her waist. It was not dark, but various shades of light brown.

This was what Karina looked like when seen from behind. The butcher had seen her mostly from behind, and had fallen in love with the body he saw in front of him in church. Her body blended in with the slender pillars supporting the vaulted ceiling. She was a pillar herself, but of flesh and blood—and no heaven, only earth.

The blacksmith loved Karina from the other side. He had looked into her large eyes that were like two windowpanes. The smith would have liked to lean against those windows and remain there the rest of his days.

Karina's eyes rarely moved, which increased the windowlike impression. It was not Karina who looked out at the world. It was the world that looked in at Karina. And this was what the smith had done, one day as he was sharpening a pair of scissors for her. He saw the play of thousands of small sparks that flew about as he sharpened the blades. He saw his own arms and barrel chest. He saw his face captured in her eyes and knew he would never get it back.

The next Sunday after mass, the smith and the butcher met in the square. They had not been friends before. But now they suddenly stopped and exchanged a long glance. Other men might possibly have conceived a hatred for each other, but not these two. They understood one another at once. The smith could see in the butcher's eyes that he wanted to die with Karina, and the butcher could see in the smith's that he wanted to live with her. They stood on opposite sides of life—or on opposite sides of Karina. They never became enemies, but they knew there was no bridge between them—for between them was a girl with immobile eyes and a mobile back.

Karina continued to live her life as before, but she knew she was living between a knife and a hammer. No one else in Ialos knew. These three—the smith, Karina, and the butcher—were the kind of people who lived with a secret and then died with it. Karina was in love with both men.

But she was in love with them the same way she was in love with her father. Day and night, his voice was always in her ear—from the day the Germans took him away.

"Good-by, my little boat!" he had said.

She had been his boat. He used to watch her as she walked in front of him, her steps unweighted as if she were gliding from one leg to the other. She would stop with an imperceptible exertion of her back, let her head drop slightly and then glide forward again. And each new stride held the beginning of the one to follow.

She moved exactly like a small boat on a long, gentle swell. Her father walked behind her, and his heart perspired with a joy that is granted only atheists, for only atheists dare thank themselves for what they have.

Karina became aware very early of the power she had over her father. A little later, she discovered her power over men in general. Karina was loved by all the men who knew her because Karina knew early how to love herself. Some of them loved her in order to destroy her. Others loved her in order to cool themselves in her shadow. Some wanted to feed her pride, others to annihilate their own.

Karina was in love with both men in exactly the same way she was in love with her dead father. She loved to walk in front of them. They could expect nothing more, for Karina would never leave her mother and never forget her father. Over the years her beauty would increase still more and songs would be written about her, but she would die like a wild rose in a deep forest, lovely and alone.

The butcher had almost stopped sleeping. He sat up nights and drank. Now Lolos, too, was gone, and the butcher was lonelier than ever. The slaughterhouse was closed, for there were no more pigs and sheep. The butcher had two empty hands and a soul that was filled to overflowing. He drank to occupy his hands and to give an outlet to the flood building up in his soul.

This immensely strong man grew thin and within a few weeks he was only half a shadow of his former self. He was constantly drunk, and children chased after him. Now and then they would hit him on the back, and when the butcher turned to stare at them in surprise they would explain that it wasn't *him* they had hit, but a fly that had landed in that particular spot. The flies had stayed with their lord. The smell of blood was still with him, although the blood itself was gone, and his strength with it.

The butcher wandered about, begged for drinks, got into arm-wrestling matches that he willingly lost in order to get a little wine from the winner. After a while he began losing even when he didn't want to. The men of the village leaped at the chance to humiliate the man they had all feared. Only the smith refused to wrestle.

The butcher didn't care if he lost to every man in the world, if only he didn't lose to the smith. But the butcher couldn't lose to the smith, because both of them had lost to Karina.

The end came rather suddenly, though not unexpectedly. One evening as the butcher was tossing down one glass of wine after the other, Josef Dog came into the tavern with two German soldiers.

They challenged the butcher to arm-wrestle. The butcher looked around like a wounded animal. He knew his strength was gone. The other customers gathered silently around his table.

"What are the stakes?" said the butcher finally.

"If you win," Josef said, "you can have free wine for a year."

"And if you win?"

"I get to ride you like a horse through the whole village."

The butcher hesitated, but the other men urged him on. "Wine for a whole year! Josef isn't as strong as he looks!" The bet was made. They sat down on opposite sides of a table, leaned forward, opened their hands, and grasped one another like pistons. Josef's face had gone pale, and the butcher gazed off through the window as if seeking strength from the earth and the trees. Then he caught sight of Karina and the smith walking side by side—not too close together, for there was fire between them, but not too far apart either. He felt the birth of a chill in his stomach, a chill that spread and attacked his guts and his arms. Josef felt the butcher's arm freeze—and give way. Josef was overjoyed. He punched the butcher and pointed to the floor. The butcher looked up. His eyes were still vacant, but the chill had melted. Now he was boiling instead. He had to strike out at someone, had to, and he hit the man who was closest. His enormous fist struck Josef in the back of the head and flung him toward the counter. The two soldiers drew their pistols, and six of their bullets bored into the butcher's dark body.

They buried the butcher beside the ten men who had been executed. Karina went to his grave every afternoon. She would gaze at it for a long time, with her father's voice in her ear saying "Good-by, my little boat."

The knife was gone. Only the hammer remained.

## THE BOMBINGS

Bombing raids became the new sensation of Ialos. It was never a question of any systematic aerial attack, only a diversionary maneuver. The Germans were supposed to believe that the Allies were preparing an invasion of Greece, whereas in fact they were planning to invade Sicily.

When the sirens sounded for the first time, no one in Ialos got particularly scared or went rushing off to the bombproof cave with the reinforced walls.

They rushed to the square instead, out of habit, and stood there staring at the sky and stretching their necks like chickens. When the Germans started firing their antiaircraft guns and the airplanes started dropping their bombs, and heaven and earth were filled with explosions that hurt their eyes and ears, the Ialites realized after all that it might be a good idea to run for the cave. But even as they ran, they took their chance to look up at the sky one last time.

It was hard for the children and old people to get to the cave. The old people had trouble running, and some of them complained loudly. "I haven't run anywhere since 1920, I don't see why . . ." and so forth.

The children could run well enough, but they couldn't resist the fireworks. The mothers would call and call, and the children would yell back that yes they were coming, and the mothers would call again, and again the children would holler they were coming, but the bombing would be over before they were all gathered in the cave.

It was at this time that Babi became famous. He was an only

child, and his mother was an only parent. She had no one else in life, and all of her love was lavished on Babi, who was sickly, intelligent, and extremely taciturn.

He used to draw pictures of everything that could be drawn on everything that could be drawn upon. His mother, whom he loved, was very strict with him, and so in spite of the fact that he was a natural soccer wing he was never allowed to play anything but goalie, which his mother considered a comparatively safe position.

This talented left wing had absolutely no desire to go into the cave. He would stand outside as if bewitched, watching the fireworks and drawing pictures of the planes. His mother would stand by the entrance to the cave and call to him in a long, drawn-out shriek: "Ba-a-a-bi-i-i!"

And he would answer "Co-o-o-mi-i-ing!" in exactly the same voice, and even the Germans would forget the war and listen to these two voices, which in some curious way contained everything that one human being could feel for another.

It became a standing joke for the whole village, including the Germans, for one person to yell "Ba-a-a-bi-i-i!" and another to answer "Co-o-o-mi-i-ing!"

Babi watched one fireworks too many. He was hit by bomb splinters that made a sieve of his head, which was rather large and had earned him the nickname "Headman" from the other boys.

The night bombings were an even greater attraction than the daytime raids. People came tumbling out of bed head over heels, which inevitably gave rise to situations that seemed designed for retelling at the cafés the following day—someone without any clothes on, someone else with a secret lover, another person's funny underwear, a couple interrupted in the midst of copulating.

The Ialites were practical people. They kept food in the cave, and blankets and lanterns. Some of them brought decks of cards or backgammon boards, and while the bombs were falling outside the people in the cave were cursing poor cards or bad throws of the dice. The women knitted socks and sweaters, and the children —those of them who were in the cave at all—hid at the back and devoted themselves to games that they otherwise had no opportunity to play.

Soon it began to feel warm in the cave, and customs started to develop. People marked out their own territories and stuck to them, though of course small disputes did arise, especially between thin people and fat ones.

The Priest, with his immense body, commandeered one entire square meter, and counting in the area that had to be left vacant around him to show a decent fear of God, the amount of space he occupied was scandalous.

"Our shepherd seems to need a whole sheepfold to himself," the Ialites muttered, crowding together as best they could.

Old Uncle Stelios was having the best days of his life. Down in the cave he could tell his stories to an audience that was grateful to hear them. Meanwhile, too, he had grown wealthy. The Germans had passed a new law requiring every Greek to have an identity card, and Uncle Stelios, who had bought a camera in the States when he was over there throwing away his money, seized the opportunity. He took up a position outside the church on Sundays and photographed the peasants in their Sunday best.

One man had bought a hat for the occasion and was absolutely shattered when Uncle Stelios informed him that he couldn't wear a hat on an identity card.

"Then you might just as well take a picture of my pig," said the indignant farmer, and Uncle Stelios said it wouldn't make any difference, the pig couldn't wear the hat either.

Uncle Stelios made piles of money. But he refused to invest it in land as his wife advised him (with that business intuition that Christians have). It seemed to Uncle Stelios that all the land he needed was a few square meters, and that much he already had. No, he preferred saving the money, and he stuffed it into empty jerry cans that he bought from the Germans and then hid away in secret places.

The money soon became worthless, because inflation reached a point where millions of drachmas wouldn't buy a crust of bread. This gave the Ialites a good laugh, and Uncle Stelios had to admit his mistake, although, as he put it, he did have "toilet paper to last a lifetime." "My ass is worth millions," he would claim later, and the joke delighted him.

One day the German antiaircraft managed to shoot down an English plane. The pilot bailed out. The Ialites watched as he floated down to earth, and the Germans waited with submachine guns. But they didn't kill him. Pilots were then, and probably still are, a kind of upper class in all armies. No one ever kills a pilot. It's the airplane they're after. The exact opposite of the Wild West, where a person wasn't allowed to shoot at the horse but the rider was fair game.

In spite of everything, the world does move forward slightly. But it never moves forward only, because every one of us, deep down inside, wants to change its direction. At some point in our lives, we all want progress to stop.

Fortunately there are very few people who manage to accomplish this, though some do. Every human being has a period when he yearns to move forward and a period when he yearns to move back.

The people of Ialos, caught up as they were in the dreadful everyday life of wartime, yearned backward rather than forward. Instead of dreaming of the new society they would build on the ruins of the war, they longed to return to the society that existed before it began.

Great catastrophes always mean a step backward in many areas. But the young people who had no past to yearn back to had to put their hopes in the future, and the future seemed to be the struggle in the mountains.

The townspeople's reactionary convictions were confirmed there in the cave, or rather their reactionary attitudes were transformed into convictions. But it was also there in the cave that the young people dreamed of a new society, and it was there in the cave, as an old war was coming to an end outside, that a new war began to take root.

# TOWARD THE END

Establishing the Security Battalions was the only smart move the Germans ever made in their effort to control the Greek people. Their other measures—arrests, forced labor, concentration camps and executions—were inadequate. The resistance only grew. But the Security Battalions might have turned things around if they had come a year earlier.

The Security Battalions were composed of Greeks who, for one reason or another, had collaborated with the Germans, and who now felt compelled to organize against the people's army.

It wasn't only the small fry who joined the Security Battalions. Prominent people like former Prime Minister Rallis, for example, and party leaders and generals and university professors supported the organization wholeheartedly.

Curiously enough, the English and Germans found themselves in agreement: they both supported the Security Battalions. The English saw them as a means of protecting their interests in Greece once the war was over. The English carried on a twofold war, at least in Greece—against the Germans and against the people's army.

It was clear that the Communists had assumed control of the resistance movement. Nevertheless, individual resistance groups included thousands of people who were not only not Communists but were actually conservative—policemen, officers, doctors, etc.

This very fact allowed the English to split the resistance or at least to organize new units that were loyal to them.

The people's army soon became a real army, with discipline and definite goals. The Security Battalions were never anything but gangs, loose aggregations of collaborators who already had a lot of blood on their hands. Of course this conflicts with the conservative version of Greek history, according to which the Communists are supposed to have committed terrible crimes and atrocities, while the Security Battalions were angels, with the royal Greek crown in their hearts.

The Security Battalions were gangs and they behaved like gangs. They burned villages, they committed indiscriminate murder, they raped and stole and plundered. As time passed and it became clearer and clearer that the Germans were going to lose the war, their Greek compatriots began acting more and more like mad dogs—mad dogs well supplied with ammunition and weapons by both the Germans and the English.

Some of their leaders were killed during the war, of course, but most of them are well-to-do citizens today. When the war was over and Greece got its first "English" government, some of them even became MPs and ministers. For this we have Churchill to thank, that great man whose memoirs are still a best-seller, to the shame of everyone still capable of feeling shame.

History is made by people. Unfortunately, it is also people who write it.

The Mayor of Ialos, whose name was Dimitreas, soon distinguished himself by the cruelty and violence of his imagination in devising new methods of executing and torturing members of the resistance—regardless of whether they were Communists.

He surrounded himself with every collaborator in Laconia. They moved from village to village and wherever they went "sisters wept and mothers mourned." Dimitreas became so famous that a foreign newspaper sent a woman reporter to visit him and write a series of articles about "the jovial captain."

Dimitreas did in fact laugh a lot, at least as long as he was allowed to continue plundering and murdering unpunished. But he wasn't allowed to continue for very long. Dimitreas and his henchmen were all wiped out at a place just outside Ialos. The place had never had a name before but afterward was always called the "Ambush."

The Germans had gone to a village on the coast where their information indicated an English submarine was going to deliver war matériel to the Resistance. Dimitreas and his gang were on their way back to Ialos from another village where they had been burning buildings and killing people.

The gangsters were in a good humor. They were singing and drinking wine that they had stolen from the peasants. They were looking forward to more fun, now that they would be able to rule Ialos and the Ialites all by themselves. They never got any farther than the Ambush.

David Kalin was there, one of the masons was there, and so were the Schoolmaster's two sons, the three brothers who had executed the German soldier, and the confectioner's two sons, who were also the partisan leaders.

The battle did not last long. Most of the gangsters were killed when their car hit a mine that the partisans had buried in the road. Dimitreas was captured and killed with two bullets, one for each eye, because, as the confectioner's sons explained, they had promised themselves to "fuck him in the eyes" some day.

Then the partisans disappeared up toward One Arm. But they left a warning in large letters:

ALL TRAITORS WILL MEET THE SAME FATE.

ELAS.

Actions of this kind were avidly discussed. Many people thought it was right to punish collaborators and gangsters. Others felt there was too great a risk of arousing family vendettas. The former group thought that people would feel secure under the protection of the people's army, the latter, that people would only be confused.

It was the latter who proved to be right. For every collaborator that was murdered, two new ones appeared, and the people grew more and more terrified. Now they were involved whether they wanted to be or not. Every family included either a collaborator or a partisan. A lot of people tried to trim their sails with the prevailing wind, and that worked fine as long as the winds relieved one another gently. But soon there were whirlwinds over the whole of Greece.

Germans, Italians, collaborators, partisans, Englishmen, and their allies. No one knew who to be afraid of. Being a Greek in those days was not easy.

When Dimitreas was liquidated, it did not take long for his family and the families of the others, with Josef Dog's help, to take revenge on the families of the partisans. The Schoolmaster's wife managed to get out of Ialos at the last moment and take Minos and Reveka to Athens by sea. But their house was burned. The mason's family was wiped out. David Kalin's second daughter, Judith, was raped and then hanged outside the town hall.

But one night the partisans came back. The confectioner's boys had given an order: "No bullets. Only knives." They took the Germans in their sleep. Not one of them escaped. Then they went to Dimitreas' brother, who was then in command of the gangsters. They dragged him out of bed.

When morning came, the partisans gathered everyone in the square. One of the confectioner's sons made a short speech.

"You see us here today, and we will be here every time we're needed. No one will escape the punishment of ELAS. But we will not hurt anyone unless they fight against us. We will not punish anyone without reason. Here we have Dimitreas' brother. He has murdered and stolen and raped. We killed his brother, but that was in battle. I ask you—what shall we do with him? I promise that your decision will be respected. Think carefully!"

The idea was that of a people's court. No one has ever come out of a people's court alive, but they didn't know that then. The crowd went silent. You could see that the peasants were thinking and thinking so intensely it almost gave them headaches, and then suddenly a woman in black shouted, "Death to the murderer!"

They all joined in. "Death to the murderer!" they shouted. "Death to the murderer!"

They were extremely conservative people condemning another extremely conservative person to death.

"So be it," said the confectioner's son.

The partisans left the town and took Dimitreas' brother with them. As they walked past his house they heard weeping, but they continued their song:

> Forward, ELAS, for Greece,
> for justice and for freedom.

The German army was not only a poor victor, lacking both generosity and understanding. It was also a poor loser. Instead of admitting defeat it plundered and pillaged and murdered right up to the end.

The Greek liberation army continued to grow. By the fall of 1943, large areas of northern Greece were under the control of ELAS. The German outposts and the Security Battalions were unable to stop them.

ELAS attracted more and more Greeks to its ranks, especially the young. Boys and girls left their homes and made their way into the hills. Eventually there were complete hospitals and schools in the liberated areas.

The first girl to disappear from Ialos was Karina the fair. Her mother had died, and the smith had disappeared. Karina had no reason to stay. No one from the village saw her again until she was captured by the Royal Army on Mount Vitsi in 1949, right at the end of the Civil War.

But a great many stories about her did reach Ialos. A beautiful girl can't disappear, not even when she dies.

The Ialites spent their days running to the square, where whoever was occupying the town at that moment would pick out their enemies and take them away. It had become routine, to the point that the Ialites (who will always survive) would ask each other when they met, "Who do you suppose they'll take today?"

A new emigration began in Greece, this time from the villages to the cities. Ialos underwent a steady depopulation, and yet there were still people left. People who had nowhere to flee. People who couldn't travel. People who did not want to die someplace else. But most of all, those who remained were the orphans. Children, who wandered around in packs and had to look out for themselves far too young.

These children would receive the English when the war was over. They would cry "He comes! He comes!" when the King was expected from England. They would live through the Civil War that followed. And finally these children would leave Ialos and Greece in order to find a new life somewhere else in the world.

We believed that the English came as liberators. In fact they were the new occupying force. The great powers were not finished with Greece. They were not finished with the Greeks, and they were not finished with Ialos.

The town had much more to go through. But of this I will tell another time. I am one of the children. Or rather, he is, to speak in the third person as Lolos always did.